Contents

WARNE COUNTY FC

1. The Squad

This is the Warne County Colts Squad getting on the coach to take us to our first away game in the Western Area Qualifying Competition for entry to the newly-formed Brontley League, Premier Division.

The idea was to get all the big clubs in the area to put their Colts teams in the same league, together with the best of the Youth Club sides from the Northern Bell and Zaniger Leagues, so we would be playing top class opposition every week, and not mucking about with tiddly teams that lost 12–0. The one with the ball is me, Napper McCann Super Star! The one standing beside me with the big grin is Ally Scott, our goalie-sub, and the big one with the broken nose is Tom Brocken, the team captain. The one with the muscles is our new signing, Robbo Robinson.

The Squad that travelled for our first game against Hume United Colts at Wickley Manor Stadium showed a few changes from the side that our Manager Davie Ledley had brought together at the beginning. We'd played half a dozen scratch games before the Qualifying Competition against nothing opposition, and things had been changed about a bit as a result.

Warne County Manager George Trotman had appointed Tommy Cowans as Coach for the Colts, because Davie Ledley was needed to look after Warne County Reserves. Their Manager had left. Davie Ledley was still overall Manager of both teams, but Tommy would coach the Colts players, and pick the team. That suited us, because Davie knew all about football and was brilliant, but he confused us with his tactical plans, and we thought Tommy would give us a bit more freedom to play.

After the scratch games Tommy decided that we were carrying too many players who wouldn't make the grade, and he cut down the Squad, leaving out three players, Reid, Bird and Zan. Reidy was one of Davie Ledley's own discoveries, and that didn't help, but Davie didn't say much. Tommy brought in one new signing of his own, Robbo Robinson, to tighten things up at the back. Robbo had played in one of the scratch games against us and, although his team lost 5–0, Tommy was so impressed that he signed him on. Tommy thought we needed strength in the team, and Robbo could link up with Tom Brocken and Ronnie Purdy to provide it.

'Going to have a team of hard men, Tommy?'

Davie said.

'Just a balance of brain and brawn!' Tommy said. 'I have to back my own judgement, Davie. I reckon this lot can do the job for me.'

Davie shrugged and went away to talk to George Trotman, which didn't make things look good for Tommy.

This is the Squad of fourteen players we were left with:

Keepers: Tony Bantam, Ally Scott.

Backs: Tom Brocken, Wally Usiskin, 'Robbo' Robinson.

Midfield: Ronnie Purdy, Nicky McCall, Joe Fish, 'Alex' Alexiou.

Strikers: Andy Jezz, Danny Mole, 'Napper' McCann, 'Matty' Matthews, Lester Singh.

That gave us fourteen players to call on for the five-match campaign, which didn't seem enough, but Tommy made it clear he was out looking for more signings, which was partly the reason for leaving three out of the Squad. We were supposed to be possible players for Warne County in the future, and Tommy said he didn't think the other three were going to be good enough. He said it wasn't fair to keep them on County's books if he didn't mean to use them and he told them to get fixed up somewhere else, and prove him wrong.

'This way everyone will get his chance,' Tommy said, but he warned us that if we couldn't do the business out on the park, we'd be out.

It was tricky for Tommy, because Warne County are one of the biggest clubs round our way. We didn't want to miss out on membership of the Premier Division of the Brontley League, but we couldn't expect to walk into it either. The Premier Division was to have twelve clubs, but more than thirty clubs had applied to play in it. Some were ruled out as no-hopers, and some because they hadn't got suitable grounds, and that left twenty-four teams. The Brontley League Foundation Committee divided the teams into four areas, Northern, Southern, Eastern and Western, with six teams in each. We had to play the other five teams in the Western Area in a round robin competition. The top three teams from the Western would go into the Premier Division, along with the top three from each of the other areas, and the teams who failed to make it would end up in Division One of the new league.

'We're going to be there!' Tommy told us. 'We've *got* to be there. My job is on the line!'

Tommy used to be a player for County. Our team's first game had been his Testimonial, after he hung up his boots. Now George Trotman, County's Manager, had made him our Coach, and if he was going to make anything of the non-playing side of the game, he had to get good results. It wasn't going to be easy, particularly with Davie Ledley breathing down his neck. Davie had helped set the team up and, although he had been put in charge of the Warne County Reserves, he still showed up from time to time. Davie has been at the club for years, and Tommy couldn't tell him to keep his nose out, even though we reckoned he wanted to.

'I don't fancy it!' my friend Joe Fish said. 'They'll have to sort out who is really in charge of this team, or we'll get nowhere.'

'Tommy is,' I said.

'Then George Trotman ought to tell Davie Ledley to back off,' Joe said.

We were both a bit nervous about it, because we only had five matches in the competition to get it right, so we couldn't afford the sort of slip-ups that might happen because there were rows going on off the field.

Davie took us for training twice when Tommy couldn't make it, and each time he got the blackboard out and started talking about patterns of play and interchanging and back marking and switch covering and stuff like that, which may have meant something to the pros who played for County, but didn't mean a lot to us.

Then Tommy would take our sessions and he talked about keeping it simple and giving it to shirt, and not worrying too much about the complicated stuff.

'The *simple* thing is that we like Tommy, and we don't like Davie!' Joe said.

'Davie yells too much,' Ally Scott, our reserve keeper said.

'Tommy yells too!' I said.

'Yeah, but you can understand what Tommy is yelling *about*,' Joe said. 'He doesn't need a blackboard and a guidebook to tell you!'

'*Liking* Tommy doesn't mean he's right,' I said.

That was the way it was when it came to the morning of the first game against Hume United Colts, and straight away we had a complication in the team.

It turned out that Wally Usiskin had banged his head on a brick wall as he fell off a ladder when he was helping his dad paint their shed. He was concussed (as well as getting covered in paint, because he was holding the paint pot when he fell) and he had to go to hospital. That was on Friday night, so Tommy didn't know he had to change the team until we all arrived to get the coach at Owen Lane, which is Warne County's home ground.

Wally's dad turned up looking very worried, and he told Davie Ledley about Wally not coming.

Davie was really mad. I thought he was going to say something rude to Mr Usiskin. His face froze, and he muttered something under his breath and turned away. He went into the office.

'Charming!' Mr Usiskin said. He's a tank of a man, built on the same scale as Wally. He went a bit red round the ears and he looked as if he was going to go after Davie Ledley and give him a piece of his mind, but Tommy Cowans nipped in first.

'Mr Usiskin?' he said. 'Tommy Cowans. Glad to meet you. That's terrible news about your youngster.'

You could see Mr Usiskin was flattered, because it isn't every day you have a famous ex-international footballer shaking your hand and asking how your son is.

Tommy Cowans is famous.

Everybody knows him. He used to play for Scotland, and Mr Hope, Headmaster at my school, Red Row Primary, says he was the fastest thing on two legs. Mr Hope knows about football and he wouldn't say it unless Tommy was really good. It was Mr Hope who recommended me to County for their Colts when the team was being set up.

Tommy dived in, telling Mr Usiskin how highly thought of Wally was and what a stabilizing influence he had on the rest of our team.

Mr Usiskin was still angry. He said something about the team *needing* a stabilizing influence if the Manager was anything to go by.

'Don't mind old Davie,' Tommy said. 'He's a headcase when it comes to football. He eats, sleeps and drinks the game and he likes everything to come out just the way he's planned it.'

'There's still no need to be rude!' Mr Usiskin said. 'My boy is in hospital with concussion, and that's more important to me than any football team.'

After Mr Usiskin had gone, Tommy went into the office. Davie Ledley and George Trotman were in there too, and they had a big confab.

Hume Colts, the team we were up against, are attached to Hume United, who are a Division below County in the Northern Combination and I think George Trotman didn't want to look silly in front of all the fans, with his Colts losing to a Colts team from a lower division.

Ally Scott came up to me.

'Looks like I'm sub!' he said, looking pleased.

We were down to thirteen players, so he had to be.

We had been playing with two main strikers, Big Matty and Danny Mole, playing down the centre of the park and Lester Singh playing wide on the left. Lester is a streak of lightning and Davie Ledley had told him *not* to cover back. We had nobody pacy on the right, so we were relying on Tom Brocken's runs coming from the back and making deep crosses from midway inside the opposition half.

That meant that Matty and Danny and Lester were our strike force, and Jezz and I had been taking turns in the scratch games to play just behind them, laying things on and picking up anything that came out of the situations they created. Tommy had talked to us both, and explained the way he saw things going. We needed height and strength in the middle, so the big two had to be in, and we needed someone who could go wide, so Lester had to be in too.

'You two are both on the small side, but you can both play and take a man on, and you know where the goal is,' he explained. 'I'm still making up my mind about who gets the nod. That doesn't mean the one who is left out should pack his boots and go home, but it does mean one of you will have to put up with being on the bench.'

'Wait and see,' Jezz said to me afterwards. 'Neither of us is sure of a place, and he has told us he is going to add to the Squad, so if we aren't in the starting team now, we could be on our way out.'

'You or me,' I said.

'Yeah,' he said. 'Haven't a hope, Napper, have you?'

He was grinning when he said it, but neither of us was grinning inside. We didn't want to be fighting each other for one place in the team, but it couldn't be helped.

Anyway, a defender was out, so a defender had to come in, which meant either Jezz or N. McCann Super Star would be on the bench. Neither of us could expect to be picked to fill Wally Usiskin's place, adding height and strength at the back, which is what Tommy said he wanted.

I thought it would be Joe Fish. Joe is the only one with the Colts Squad who goes back to my days with the Red Row Stars. He was Captain of the Stringy Pants, St Gabriel's, and they were our big rivals. Joe is a good player, with great positional sense, but he is on the small side, and he likes to make runs forward when he can, instead of sticking at the back covering for other people, which is what Tommy had been asking Wally to do in our friendlies.

Tommy didn't pick Joe Fish.

Instead, he switched the whole thing round at the last moment, moving Danny Mole back from striker into Wally's position at the back to give our defence some weight and strength.

Jezz and I were both in!

I thought I might get moved up to partner Big Matty, but instead Tommy brought in Jezz to play alongside Matty, and left me still in the back-up role.

Jezz looked delighted. He'd turned up expecting to compete with me for a place on the subs' bench, and now he was leading the attack!

Danny Mole didn't like the switch into defence. I thought he was going to tackle Tommy about it, but our Captain, Tom Brocken, muttered something to him, and he said, 'OK, Boss!'

'Right! Well, everybody on the bus!' Davie Ledley said, and we all got on.

Joe Fish sat at the back, apart from the rest of us, until Tommy shifted seats and went to talk to him. Tommy is good that way. He spots when someone is feeling fed up. By picking Danny to play at the back it looked as if Tommy was saying Joe would never get his place in the team. Joe must have thought that he might as well pack it in.

That started me thinking about my own game.

Jezz had got Danny Mole's place, leading the

attack alongside Matty, which would give him a chance to look good. One of us would be dropped when Danny came back into the forward line for the next match, and it looked as if it would be me.

Unless I played out of my skin, and got a hat trick coming in from behind, or something. Then Jezz would be on the bench, and I would hold my place.

So all I had to do was score a hat trick in our first Western Area Qualifier!

WICKLEY MANOR STADIUM LTD

HUME COLTS

v.

WARNE COUNTY COLTS

Brontley League: Western Area Qualifying Competition

KO 11 a.m.

PRODUCTION OF THIS PROGRAMME SPONSORED BY

THE BRONTLEY BUILDING SOCIETY

TODAY'S TEAMS

HUME COLTS (Green & white hoops, white shorts) **V.** **Warne County Colts** (Black & white stripes, black shorts)

HUME COLTS		Warne County Colts
From:		From:
Jackson	1	Bantam
Smit (J.)	2	Robinson
Peters	3	Usiskin
Spencer	4	Purdy
Darnley	5	Brocken
Smit (T.)	6	Alexiou
Hamsworth	7	McCall
Foley	8	Singh
Olney	9	Matthews
Stewart	10	Mole
Macmor	11	~~McGann~~ Mc Cann!
Hunter	12	Jezz
Rice	14	Fish
	15	Scott

MATCH OFFICIALS

Ref:
B. Simms.

Linesmen:
O. Oakes, B. Walsh

Today's match at Wickley Manor marks the Hoops' opening fixture in the Western Area Qualifying Competition. The Hoops' visitors are Warne County Colts and an interesting match should result, if the old rivalries between the two clubs at a more senior level are anything to go by!

WELCOME TO THE BRONTLEY LEAGUE!

Notes by 'Stroller'

The Hoops are proud to be involved in yet another competition, but this one has an important difference.

For the past eight years, Hoops junior sides have competed (with variable success!) in the Zaniger League and other competitions organized locally, but when Manager Mike Stymson was approached pre-season by the organizers of the new Brontley League, he felt the opportunity it would offer for the development of the young 'stars' of tomorrow was too great to resist.

Briefly, the new league will involve a number of newly-formed Colts sides attached to the Senior clubs in the area, plus the best of the Youth sides at present competing in the Zaniger League and the Northern Bell League.

The new League will have three Divisions (Premier, First and Second) of twelve teams each.

Today's game is our first fixture in the Qualifying Competition designed to 'sort out' the twenty-four clubs who wish to enter the Premier Division of the new league. Clubs have been divided, on a geographical basis, into four groups of six. The Hoops are in the Western Area with today's visitors Warne County, and with Swanley, Wolverton, Olympic YC and Queenstown; each team will meet the others once. The top three teams in each Area will compete in the Brontley League Premier Division when the League commences next season. The remaining twelve clubs will play in the First Division, and the Second Division will be made up from clubs in the existing leagues.

Mike would like to pay tribute to the Brontley Building Society's generous gesture in providing sponsorship to the Burnswicke Community Association for the organization of the new venture, and, in particular, for their financial assistance in producing match programmes for each game – a real innovation at this level!

BRONTLEY LEAGUE
WESTERN AREA QUALIFYING COMPETITION

First Series Fixtures

OLYMPIC YC	v.	WOLVERTON
SWANLEY	v.	QUEENSTOWN
HUME UNITED COLTS	v.	WARNE COUNTY COLTS

NEXT MATCH AT THE MANOR!

Hume Ladies v. Old Valley Owls WFC
This Sunday KO 3 p.m. sharp!
Bring the family!

SOCIAL CLUB NOTES

Tonight (Saturday):
IVANHOE AND THE CRUSADERS
Doors open 8 p.m.

Wednesday:
MEMBERS BINGO
75p per card. 7.30 p.m.

Next Saturday:
CAR BOOT SALE
9.30 a.m. in the car-park
(In aid of Wickley & Brompton Senior Citizens Fund)

BE THERE! BUY AND SELL IN A GOOD CAUSE!

2. Hume United Colts v. Warne County Colts

This was the Warne County Colts line-up for our first match in the Western Area Qualifying Competition, against Hume United Colts at the Wickley Manor Stadium:

Bantam
Brocken Robinson Alexiou Mole McCall
Purdy McCann
Matthews Jezz Singh
Subs: Scott, Fish

That is how it looked on paper, and we reckoned it was a good team and had every chance of getting the points. Tommy said in his team talk that he was sure we would win, but things look *different* when you get out on the field.

It wasn't Wembley. It was Wickley Manor Stadium, which is where Hume United play their Reserve and Youth Team matches. It is a proper stadium with a small grandstand, a social club round the side and a running track, because it is owned by Wickley Athletic's club.

I haven't played on a pitch with a running track round it before. It felt odd. We were a long way from the crowd . . . well, what crowd there was. Most of them were in the grandstand. There must have been about two hundred mums and dads, grannies and grandads and a few Hume maniacs who were at our game and would go to the First Team game in the afternoon. There were four of them with a Hume flag which had HOOPS FOR GLORY written on it. They must have felt a bit silly. They were sitting on the terrace behind one of the goals.

My mum was there. My dad couldn't come because he was off being interviewed about a job somewhere but Mum said she wasn't going to miss it and she got a lift with Mr Hope. They weren't in the stand. They were down behind one of the dug-outs with George Trotman, the Manager of County. Mr Hope and George Trotman seemed to be great mates.

Daniel Rooney and Dribbler from school had told me they were coming too, if they could, but I couldn't see them, so I thought maybe they hadn't come.

It was all right though, because there were free programmes that advertised the Brontley Building Society. It was the first-ever time I have had my name in a real match programme, even if they did spell it 'McGann' not 'McCann', and I was very pleased because it meant I could show it to everybody at school and my dad. My mum got a programme as well and that meant we would have two, one to show the people at school, and one for my Football Career Book. My Football Career Book was Miss Fellow's idea. She said I should keep it and put things about the games I played in it. She said it would help my English. She is a really good teacher but she does her shopping on Saturday mornings so she wasn't able to come all the way over to Wickley, though she said she would make a big effort to come and see me play when we had our next home game.

We were out too early.

Hume kept us waiting.

The ref and the linesmen came out and the linesmen came down and inspected the nets and then there was a lot of shouting from the stands and Hume were out on the field.

They had green and white hoop shirts, like Glasgow Celtic, which is why they are called the Hoops.

Then the ref looked at his watches (he had three of them, all strapped to his left arm). He blew his whistle and Tom Brocken, our Captain, ran up to the middle and tossed with their Captain, who was a big guy called Darnley wearing the Number 5 shirt.

Tom Brocken won the toss, and we were playing into the railway end of the ground, which meant their keeper, Jackson, had the sun in his eyes. Davie Ledley and Tommy had agreed that that was what we should do if we won the toss. The idea was that we would sling a few high ones in out of the sun, and unsettle the keeper early on.

We lined up, and their centre, Spencer, kicked off.

They played the ball all the way back to the keeper, and straight away he lofted a high ball out to their left wing.

Tom Brocken went for it with their left-winger, a tiny guy called Rice.

Tom climbed all over him!

Free kick!

Davie Ledley was up out of the dug-out yelling at Tom, and we hadn't even started. Tom just shrugged and ran back.

Darnley came up from the back, and took the free. It was from just inside our half, on their left and we thought he might do what we had been going to do, and throw a high one in to test our keeper, before Tony Bantam had got a chance to handle the ball. He shaped to do that, but instead he played the ball square to their Number 8, who had moved inside. I should have been picking him up, but I had dropped back, thinking that Tony might have to come out and punch clear and I could gather the ball. Matty was our only player who had stayed up, but he didn't move after the Number 8, and suddenly the Number 8 was in his stride, just coming out of the centre circle, unmarked.

Tony shouted 'Out' from the back, and everybody moved forward, which is what we'd been told to do. The idea was that when the Number 8 released the ball they would be caught offside.

They would have been, if he had.

Instead the Number 8 headed straight at Nicky McCall, who had spotted what was happening quicker than everybody else. He put Nicky the wrong way, and dummied Ronnie Purdy, who was left crash-tackling the air, and suddenly he was clean through the middle of the defence in a solo dribble, with everybody caught out of position because of trying to play the offside.

Tony Bantam came off his line like a rocket and committed himself in a full-length dive. Their Number 8 steered round him and managed to keep his feet, but he pushed the ball just too far. He could have played it back into the path of his forwards but instead he went for death or glory and tried to steer the ball into the net from an almost impossible angle.

The ball whammed into the side-netting, just the wrong side of the post.

This shows what happened:

First, the initial run by the Number 8, whom nobody had picked up because we were expecting the long ball.

C: Colts pushing up for offside

The important thing is that we all rushed out, to make the other forwards offside. When the Number 8 kept on running everybody was moving the wrong way, so that he had the advantage of surprise.

The next picture shows what the Number 8 *should* have done when he had rounded Tony but ended up with a bad angle on goal, and what he *did* do:

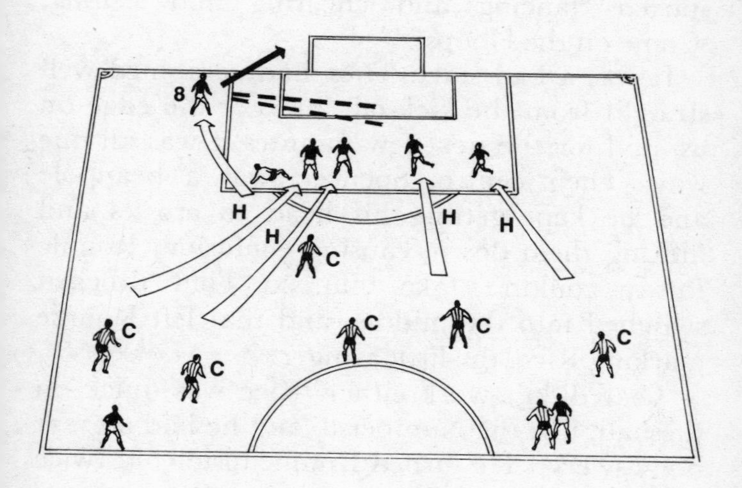

C: Stranded Colts expecting offside decision

H: Hume players following up

It was a let-off!

'Your man, Napper!' Nicky McCall grunted to me, as we moved upfield for the goal-kick.

I nodded. He was right, but I wasn't the only one who had been caught out.

Their Captain, Darnley, was shouting and clapping, and they were all perked up by the near miss. The Hume fans with the banner had been trudging up from the railway end to get behind our goal when it happened and they started dancing and cheering and yelling, 'Come on the Hoops!'

It was a bad start. They had combined well straight from the kick-off, and got the edge on us, and for the next few minutes it was all one way. Their centre, Spencer, was a beanpole and he kept getting his head to crosses and flicking them down, causing confusion. Ronnie Purdy couldn't take him, so Tom Brocken switched into the middle, and that left Ronnie marking Rice, the little winger.

That didn't work either. Rice was quick on the ball, like the Number 8, and he had a great body swerve. He turned Ronnie inside out twice in succession, and the second time Ronnie went in really heavily, to try and show him who was who. Ronnie got the yellow card, and gave away a free kick in a dangerous position, just at the corner of the box. Their Captain, Darnley, the big Number 5, moved into our box alongside Spencer. Big Matty moved back to cover him, signalling me to lie upfield, in the hope of a quick break. Rice picked himself up, and placed the ball for the free kick. This time it was obvious what they were going to do, and they did it.

Rice played a high outswinger and Darnley and Spencer both went for it with Tom Brocken and Matty. Darnley ran towards the near post at the last moment, taking Matty with him, but the ball was flighted to the far post, where Spencer had made himself space by dropping off Tom. Danny Mole saw what was happening, and tried to cover it, but he was too late. The ball went over Tom, and it was dropping for Spencer, but Tony Bantam came off his line and made a full-length diving catch.

It was a really brilliant save! Tony had read the ball perfectly and managed to hold on to it, but we knew we couldn't rely on him getting it right every time, and he had already prevented two certain goals, once with the catch, and before that by being so fast off his line when they beat the offside.

Tony threw the ball out to me. It was an awkward ball, coming chest high, and I was on the edge of the centre circle, facing our goal, with their Number 5 pounding up behind me. 'Alex' Alexiou had come racing out of our box, and my first idea was to play the ball back to him, and go on a run, hoping he would make a quick return pass, but then I caught sight of Lester Singh. He was all on his own, racing inside.

I moved towards the ball, with the Number 5 closing in on me and then, at the last moment, I ducked and back-headed the ball over the Number 5, just before he cannoned into me.

The ball spiralled in the air and dropped right in Lester's path. Darnley and the other defenders had all come upfield for the free, with just the Number 5 holding back to cover me. Singhy was under orders to use his pace, and his marker had drifted forward, so Singhy was in the clear when I back-headed the ball.

He took the ball in his stride and motored straight for goal. The keeper came haring out of his area but he had misjudged Lester's pace. Lester had time to knock the ball casually past the keeper, skip over his desperate dive, and poke the ball into the empty net from about fifteen metres!

GOAL! GOAL! GOAL! GOAL!

Then Lester did a somersault, and came up with both hands punching the air at the crowd . . . only there wasn't a crowd behind the goal, just four little kids.

We were 1–0 up out of nothing when they had done all the attacking and we hadn't even had the sniff of an attack!

It is the kind of thing that often can happen when a team is right on top and their defenders start roaming upfield to cash in.

What happened next was even more extraordinary.

They took the centre, and Spencer passed to the Number 10, who slipped it back to big Darnley. Darnley was looking pretty disgusted, and he toyed with the ball for a moment, as Jezz came rushing at him. Then he lobbed it back towards the keeper.

He lobbed it short, and Jezz kept on running. It looked as if there was nothing on. The keeper started off his line and their Number 4 reached the ball in front of Jezz. It bounced high, and the Number 4 had to stretch to head it back with Jezz hustling him.

He nodded it towards the keeper, but he misheaded, and instead of the ball landing in the keeper's arm it flew right over him and bounced twice, before ending in the net.

GOAL!

2–0 to us!

Two goals in a minute, and completely against the run of play. We had been back-pedalling like mad, hardly able to get the ball out of our area, and now we were two goals up, and winning the match!

The keeper walked back and fished the ball out of the net. Big Darnley stood there with his hands on his hips and his head down and everybody was mobbing Jezz. He hadn't actually touched the ball, but he had made the goal all the same by chasing after what looked like a totally lost cause and forcing the defenders into making errors.

Their heads were down, but they were a good team, and they didn't pack it in.

Darnley started waving people about, yelling at his defenders to tighten up, but he had learnt his lesson. He dropped right back off Matty, because he knew they couldn't afford another mistake, which would put the game out of reach. The Number 5 moved up tight on me, and the Number 6 closed Jezz down and the Number 2, who had been caught out on the wrong side of Singhy for the first goal, went firmly into the back pocket and stayed there.

We got some play, because Alex started pushing up, and Matty was roaming about, but we didn't make much of it as the marking was pretty stiff. Tom Brocken got away twice on the right but he wasted his centres both times.

Big Spencer had a run or two down the middle, but Ronnie had switched positions again with Tom Brocken, and he was cutting Spencer out of it. Rice, who had been troubling both Ronnie and Tom, collected a kick on the ankle from Ronnie in a fifty-fifty tackle, and he drifted out of it.

We were 2–0 up, and holding them, though Danny Mole got caught once or twice at the back. He was strong, but he isn't used to the position, and he kept playing people onside by not moving up quickly enough. Ronnie started yelling at him, and then Tom Brocken yelled at Ronnie, and Tommy and Davie Ledley came off the bench and yelled at them both and the ref stopped the game and went over and gave Davie a touch-line talking-to.

That wasn't good, but the important thing was that we were holding them. They looked good when they were coming at the opposition bang, bang, bang, but they didn't know how to slow things down and change the tempo when things were running against them.

A team that likes to attack is often at a disadvantage when things go wrong, because of the danger of conceding more breakaways. They could have been two or three goals up, and instead they were trailing by two, and they hadn't sorted out what to do about it. The Number 8, who had nearly sprung our offside in the very first minute, started trying to do things on his own again, but Robbo had him sorted out and by half-time Tony had only had another two shots to deal with, although he had picked up a warning from the ref about disputing an offside. Tony was *right* and the ref was *wrong*, but it was still a stupid thing to do.

2–0 when we went into the dressing-room.

Tommy was supposed to be our Coach, but Davie Ledley got into the dressing-room before him, and started reading everybody a lecture. From the way he went on, you would have thought we were 2–0 down!

He kept yacking about not marking, and how we had all forgotten how to play the offside.

He seemed to have offside on the brain.

'It's Danny!' Ronnie Purdy said, when we'd had about two minutes of where's-your-offside-trap. 'It isn't his fault. He's out of position, and he's getting caught.'

Davie rounded on him. 'You!' he said. 'You are lucky still to be on the field, after the treatment you handed out to the little fellow.'

He meant Rice, who had been dancing round our defenders, before he was kicked.

'I'm supposed to be a ball-winner!' Ronnie said.

'Then go and win it!' Davie said. 'That doesn't mean diving in and lifting people!'

'You're looking good, lads!' was all Tommy got the chance to say.

Then we had to go out again.

'You'd think we were losing, not winning!' Jezz said to me as we came out of the tunnel.

Davie had warned us that things would be different in the second half, because the Hume Manager would have sorted his team out. They were 2–0 down in a game they could have been winning, and they'd taken the pressure off us because they were afraid of making more mistakes after the second goal. By hanging back, they had let us sit on our lead.

'You've got to hold them for the first fifteen minutes,' Davie said. 'Do that, and the game's ours!'

They came out for the second half and tore into us, right from the kick-off.

Spencer fired one over when he was clear, after Danny had played him onside for the umpteenth time. Then Tony tipped a curler from the Number 11 on to his crossbar, and Ronnie Purdy cleared off the line. The Number 8 managed to give Nicky McCall the slip and would have been clean through, but he tried to turn Nicky a second time, and Robbo got him when he overran the ball.

Rice had got his legs back, and started wandering. He turned up on the other flank, where they had spotted that Danny Mole was having a bad day, and he turned Danny three times in succession, without managing to get a decent cross in.

Ten minutes gone, and we were still holding them, but we were struggling.

Then Tom Brocken got clear on the right. Alex slipped the ball to him, just short of the half-way line.

Matty made a run for the area, anticipating a long ball, and Darnley went with him. Jezz laid off, and the right back, spotting him free on the edge of the area, came off Singhy, and then hesitated, not wanting to commit himself.

Tom hit a long cross. I think it was meant for Matty, but it was over-hit. Matty went up with Darnley, hoping to glance the ball to Jezz, but it beat both of them, just grazing the top of

Darnley's head. The touch was enough. It lifted the ball over the right back and there was Singhy racing in, unmarked, at the far post.

GOAL!

Another goal out of nothing! They had done nearly all the attacking, and we were 3–0 up.

Tommy Cowans was doing a dance with Davie Ledley! Then Davie started yelling at everybody to concentrate, and the ref came over and warned him again. It didn't seem to matter much! Nobody paid any attention because we knew we had our first match won!

3–0, and we would have 3 points from the first game and maybe we would top the table if nobody did any better than three goals, and then we would be a sure thing to qualify for the

Premier Division. We all knew we wouldn't be a sure thing, because there were still four games left to play in our section, but that is what it felt like.

Tommy told Joe Fish to get warmed up, and Joe began running up and down on the track, looking hopeful.

Hume were going to pieces!

The defenders were shouting at their keeper for not cutting the ball out and he was slanging big Darnley for not getting his header in, and the back who had moved off Singhy to cover Jezz was looking sick, because Singhy had scored two of our three goals and the back would probably never be picked again.

Darnley kept cool. He started talking to his team, and they pulled things together a bit, and got back into it. It was their Manager's turn to get a telling-off from the ref for touch-line coaching, because he was up waving his arms about and telling his team to push forward.

That's what they did. 2–0 down, and there was still a point in defending, but 3–0 down with half an hour to go left them with no alternative but to pitch into us.

Rice was all over the place, twisting and turning and pulling people out of position.

Ronnie went for him on the edge of the box, and Rice went down like a ninepin. Ronnie caught him outside the box, but Rice fell in it, and they all howled for a penalty. The ref, Mr Simms, gave it, and Ronnie ran up and started shouting and the ref pulled the red card! I don't know whether Ronnie was sent off for backchat to the ref, or whether it was for a last-man tackle, or persistent fouling, but he was off, so it didn't make any difference what it was for.

Ronnie was off, and Tony Bantam had no chance with the spot kick, which Rice took himself, grinning all over his face.

3–1 to us.

Tommy put Joe Fish on, and pulled Danny Mole off. It was reasonable, because Danny had been caught out of position so much. I was relieved, because I thought I might have been the one to come off, if he had wanted Danny to switch back up front.

Then they got a corner and Tony Bantam went for it with big Darnley. It looked as if Darnley put his elbow across Tony and we thought we should have had a free for barging or obstruction, but instead the ball banged off Darnley's shoulder and Joe Fish coming off the line stuck out his foot to clear the ball and only managed to turn it into the roof of our net.

It was the first time Joe had touched the ball since he came on the pitch, and he had scored a goal against us. He stood there with his hands on his head, looking sick. Joe had positioned himself well, reading the game better than

Danny would have. Danny would never have got near it ... I bet Joe wished he hadn't either!

3–2 to us, and ten minutes to go, and Tony Bantam got a talking to for arguing with the ref about being obstructed.

'Keep your shape! Keep your shape!' Davie Ledley was yelling from the line, but he didn't say how we were supposed to keep our shape with the whole Hume team going mad and coming at us.

Ronnie was off, and that left us with a big hole at the back which Robbo was trying to fill, but he was struggling because Joe hadn't recovered from the OG and kept missing his tackles. Then Tom Brocken switched Robbo to take the centre again, because Spencer was winning everything in the air.

Spencer still won everything.

Five minutes to go.

Still 3–2 to us, down to ten men, and hoofing the ball away to nobody, because Lester Singh had faded right out with no one to feed him the ball, and Jezz was stranded up on the centre spot, being a spectator.

A big high ball into the area.

Tony came out to catch it, the way he had been taking balls all afternoon, but the ball was coming right out of the sun and Tony got underneath it.

Spencer came charging at him as he went up and Tony, realizing he had come too far for the catch, tried to back-pedal and punch.

Next minute they were both lying in the net, and so was the ball.

It should have been a free for charging in on the keeper, but the ref blew his whistle and pointed to the centre spot.

'Noooo! Ref!' Tony yelled.

Out came the red card.

Robbo fished the ball out of the net and booted it, and it hit the little Number 8, who went down as if he had been pole-axed.

Another red card!

3–3, and we had three men sent off, so we were down to eight, with Matty taking Tony's jersey and going in goal, while the Hume physio was busy trying to get the Number 8 on to his feet.

Davie Ledley and Tommy had come on to help the physio, and when the Number 8 was standing up rubbing his head, Davie Ledley said something to the ref.

Another red card!

I didn't think you could give a Manager a red card, but the ref did. Davie stood there glaring at him while all the Hume fans were roaring. Then Davie turned round and trudged off the pitch.

He went to the dug-out but the linesman

flagged and the ref came over and ordered him out of the dug-out as well.

That was it.

Nothing else happened.

We held out the last few minutes and then the whistle went and we headed for the touch-line.

'The ref cost us the match!' Tommy Cowans said disgustedly as we came off. 'Two points down the drain!'

He was right.

All three of their goals weren't goals. The penalty kick was for an offence outside the box, and the other two should have been free kicks for going at the goalie. Instead of giving us free kicks, he had sent three of our team off, plus ordering the Manager out of the dug-out.

Still, 3–3. We hadn't lost.

We were still in the competition with a shout.

'If we can find enough players to field a team next week!' Tom Brocken said, when we were in the dressing-room.

Three sendings-off meant three automatic one-match suspensions, and Wally was on the sick and injured list, so the fourteen players we'd started with were down to ten.

'Tommy should never have left us with such a small squad!' Lester Singh said. 'Now look what has happened. We draw this one, and we lose next week because we can't put a proper team out, and we'll almost be out of the race!'

Everybody was down in the mouth, even Ally, who should have been pleased, because at least he was certain of getting a game in place of Tony.

With no Ronnie or Robbo at the back, it looked as if he would be busy anyway.

'I don't think that ref only cost us two points,' Joe said, when we were on our way back to Owen Lane in the coach. 'I reckon he's cost us five, with the sendings-off.'

How could we win our next game with three defenders missing?

3. Crisis!

'Napper?' Miss Fellows said.

'Yes, Miss?'

She was up at her desk, and she was looking at my Football Career Book.

'What's all this, Napper?' she said. 'I want this book kept sensibly as a record of your football. It's not a game you know!'

'Miss?' I said. 'Football *is* a game, Miss.'

'The book,' she said. 'It is supposed to be a serious part of your school work, for assessment. That means you have to be sensible.'

I didn't say anything. I didn't know what she was on about. I had written trillions about the game against the Hoops, and that was what she'd said she wanted me to do.

'"The ref was a rat",' she read out, and everybody started giggling. She frowned and looked very serious, and everybody stopped giggling except Ugly Irma, who never can stop. She goes red and quakes when she tries to.

'"The ref was a rat" is not the sort of thing I want in this book, Napper,' she said.

'Well, he was, Miss,' I said. 'He gave three bad goals and he sent nearly our whole team off and now they are suspended and they won't be able to play in the next match and I don't know whether our Manager will be allowed to coach us, because he was ordered off the pitch too.'

'I'm sure your referee was doing his best, Napper,' Miss Fellows said. 'You can't go round saying things like that about people who give their time to help you with your football.'

'I didn't say it, Miss,' I said.

'It's in your book,' she said, tapping the page. 'If *you* didn't say it, who did?'

'Mr Hope, Miss,' I said.

Then everybody started laughing, even Miss Fellows, although she tried to look as if she wasn't, but then she gave up.

The trouble was, it wasn't funny.

It meant we had one player on the injured list, Wally Usiskin, and three players suspended, Ronnie Purdy, Tony Bantam and Robbo Robinson. They are three of our best players and we had a big game coming up against Wolverton. Wolverton's First Team are a Division above Warne County in the Northern Combination so we thought their Youth Team would be a lot better than Hume's, and now we had to face them with only ten players to pick from, and our Manager suspended as well.

The referee *was* a rat. If we lost the Wolverton

game because of our missing players we would have only one point from the draw against Hume out of two games, and our chances of making the Premier Division would be almost gone.

I told Mr Hope about it in the car, going over to training. He told me after school he would give me a lift, if I liked. I was surprised, because I'd been meaning to go on the bus and I didn't know what he was going for.

'I've been co-opted,' he said.

'What to?' I said.

'Assistant to your new Manager!' he said.

'What new Manager?'

'Tommy Cowans,' he said. 'Your Coach has been promoted! Davie Ledley was so disgusted after Saturday's game that he told George Trotman he didn't want any more to do with it. So he's out, and I am in. Manager's Assistant and Chief Scout. Part-time and unpaid of course. It means I can also be your taxi-driver and get you to the ground after school on training nights, so you should be pleased!'

I think he thought Tommy would manage us better too.

We thought Tommy might have brought down some new players to sign on so that we could field a team on Saturday, but there was no sign of anybody. Lester said a mate of his called Hasty had been approached, but he wasn't going to sign for us because he had heard we were a dirty team.

'Three men sent off!' Lester said.

That didn't please anybody.

Training was much the same as usual.

It was wet, so we didn't get any ball-work. Tommy took us in the gym and we did circuit training and then he read us all a lecture about keeping our cool in the game, *especially* when the decisions went against us, and particularly about dissent. He said he didn't agree with all the ref's decisions, particularly the one against Tony, but we simply couldn't afford to have players sent off for nothing.

'I should never have *been* sent off!' Tony grumbled.

'You had a go at the ref on the second goal, *and* the penalty!' said Tommy. 'He gave you *three* chances. You pushed him too far, protesting on the third one!'

'Every time there was an important decision, it went against us!' Tom Brocken said. 'I reckon the ref should have had a green and white shirt.'

That is what we all thought, but it didn't do any good. Tommy lectured us some more about dissent and he gave Ronnie Purdy a going-over for making wild tackles. He said the only one he had any sympathy for was Robbo, who had never meant to floor their player when he booted the ball out of our net after the third goal.

'The ref read that one wrong,' he said, 'but that is the kind of thing that happens, particularly when a game has begun to get out of control. The ref over-reacted, but it would never have happened if you had all kept your cool, and not let the situation develop. As it is, you let it slip, and we have lost two points, not to mention creating a few selection problems for the next game.

I didn't think there could be many problems, because we only had ten players to pick from, so it was everybody already in the team plus somebody's-granny-who-owned-a-pair-of-boots.

'We're looking for new recruits,' Tommy said, when somebody asked him about the team. 'It is obvious that the balance of the side isn't right, even with a full squad. So I won't be announcing the team until just before the match, in the hope that the Chief Scout can come up with something!'

He meant Mr Hope.

Mr Hope hadn't stayed around for training. After he let me off at the players' entrance he had gone into the office with George Trotman and Tommy. They had a talk and then Mr Trotman and Mr Hope went off in Mr Hope's car, and Tommy came in to us.

Mr Hope still hadn't showed up by the time we had finished training and had our showers, so I was left hanging around at the ground, waiting for my lift home.

It was nearly ten o'clock when they got back, which meant I was in dead trouble because I was supposed to be in by nine, but I thought it would be all right because it was Mr Hope's fault, not mine.

Tommy and Mr Hope and George Trotman all went into the office, and they talked and they talked and they talked, and it was almost half-ten before Mr Hope remembered about me and came out to drive me home.

He didn't say much in the car at first.

The only big news was that Wally definitely wouldn't be playing on Saturday. Mr Usiskin had made a dreadful fuss and written a letter complaining to George Trotman about Davie Ledley's attitude. Mr Hope and George Trotman had gone over to speak to him and sort it out, but Mr Usiskin wasn't going back on what he had said in his letter, so that meant Wally wouldn't be playing for us again. Mr Usiskin had made George Trotman cancel his registration as a County Colts player.

'That means we'll only have ten men, Saturday,' I said.

'Not *exactly*,' Mr Hope said. 'The Chief Scout has had a busy night!' He was grinning all over his face. 'There is no harm in telling you now, because you'll find out soon, anyhow!'

'Telling me what?' I said.

'What are we short of?' he said.

'Players!' I said, because that was obvious.

'Tommy is trying to build a team,' he said. 'Not just any team, a good one, that will be able to perform respectably in the Premier Division, if we qualify for it. What do you think the present team needs?'

I thought about it.

'Somebody to go wide on the right,' I said. 'Tom Brocken is all over the place, and when he makes his runs from the back the team is all out of balance.'

'Y-e-s,' Mr Hope said. '*You* might fill that role, or young Jezz could be given a run. We have both of you competing for the same slot at the moment, and that is a luxury a small squad can't afford. Switching one of you on to the right should solve that problem.'

I thought about it. I didn't fancy it myself, and I didn't think Jezz would either. Both of us wanted one of the two up-front striker positions, and being put out of position going wide didn't seem to be a good way to go about displacing Danny Mole or Matthews.

'Forget about your own worries, Napper,' Mr Hope said. 'What does the team need? Who would you be trying to sign in a hurry, if you were the Manager?'

'Two defenders,' I said. 'We're two short.'

'That is just for next week,' he said. 'There's no point in bringing in some lad for one game.

Supposing we weren't two men short, what would improve the team?'

'Somebody to lay on the through balls,' I said. We had stacks of players who wanted to move through on the ball, but nobody (apart from Tom Brocken) who had much idea of playing the ball directly out of defence and into the danger spots, so that the forwards could run on to it.

'Right! Right! Right!' he said. 'Now, it seems to me that not so long ago there was a team round here which had a player who could do that!'

It took me a minute to grasp what he meant.

'Harpur Brown!' I said. Harpur was the player who moved the ball about in the Red Row Stars team, when we had one. The Stars depended on him, and when he went on to his new school we weren't able to field a team any more, which is how I ended up being recommended to County for their Colts. Harpur has a brilliant footballing brain, and I could see how he would fit in. It would be great playing with him again, because we link up really well, and with Harpur laying some balls on for me I might get a chance to score some goals for a change.

'And Cyril,' he said, looking very pleased with himself.

'Cyril?' I gasped.

Cyril Small, the Red Row cruncher. Cyril

was another one who had moved on to a new school, though I wasn't sure which one. I hadn't seem him at all for months because his family had moved over to Blaxton.

Harpur to do the scheming, Cyril to do the sound tackling and covering at the back. They had been the mainsprings of the Red Row Stars, and maybe they could do it for County as well, if they fitted in.

'It will be like a Red Row Old Boys team!' Mr Hope said, laughing.

It would . . . if Harpur and Cyril could bring it off. They were both brilliant when we were the Red Row Stars, but then we were playing against other school teams, and I had already found out that playing for the County Colts was much tougher. I thought Harpur could probably manage it, but Cyril had good Cyril days and bad Cyril days, and he relied a lot on being strong in the tackle. That was OK with some of the titches we played against for Red Row, but I thought he might not be able to do it for the Colts.

'Will they be in the team on Saturday?' I asked.

'That's up to Tommy,' he said. 'I've staked my new Chief Scout reputation on them, but Tommy hasn't seen them play. I don't know if he'll want to risk it! He's got his eye on several players.'

If Harpur and Cyril signed it meant we had twelve players to choose from for the game against Wolverton Colts, which was a game we absolutely had to win if we were to keep in touch with the leaders. That is the trouble with a round robin competition, where you only play each team once. Lost ground at the start would be impossible to make up. We had only one point when we should have had three, and if Wolverton beat us we would have one point out of a possible six, with only three games to go. Our chance of making the Premier Division would be almost gone.

It was the kind of important game we should have gone into with a settled team and a pattern of play, and instead we looked like going into it with a patched-up team, minus our star goalie and our two main ball-winners, and with two new players who hadn't even seen our team play.

I decided that we would all have to play out of our skins if we were going to get the result we needed!

I was just getting excited about it, when I realized that we had twelve players available, and I *might* not be in the team. If Tommy brought Danny Mole back in to lead the attack and played Cyril and Harpur to replace Robbo and Ronnie Purdy, somebody was going to have to drop out. If it was a defender, it would be Joe Fish or Nicky

McCall. If it was an attacker, it would be me or Jezz, and I thought it might be me, because I had only done one good thing in the game, setting up Singhy for the first goal. Jezz had shown a lot, playing down the middle, and he'd made the second goal by chasing Darnley's silly back-pass.

Maybe having Cyril and Harpur added to the Warne County Squad wasn't such a good idea after all. Harpur would lay on brilliant balls for Jezz, and I would never get back in the team. If I wasn't in the team when we only had twelve to choose from, how could I hope to make it when the other three came back from suspension, and we had fifteen?

Maybe I would be in the team, and Jezz would be out.

It was a big maybe!

OWEN LANE STADIUM

WARNE COUNTY COLTS

v.

WOLVERTON

Brontley League: Western Area Qualifying Competition

KO 11 a.m.

NOTES FROM OUR CHAIRMAN, Mr Duncan Murphy

Today's match, marking the home debut of our Colts side in a competitive fixture, is an exciting expansion in my plans for the development of Warne County. It is my personal conviction that the future of this club lies in building deeper links with the community. Giving our local schoolboys their chance to shine at the Lane is part and parcel of that process. I know that all you dads (and mums) will turn out to give the lads a cheer this morning!

Yours, in football,
Duncan Murphy

TOMMY SAYS...

The Colts kicked off with a hard-fought draw against our old rivals Hume, at Wickley Manor, in a match which was dominated by some controversial refereeing decisions. The Colts cruised to a 3–0 lead with two goals by L. Singh and an OG brought about by Andy Jezz's robust follow-up in a lost cause. Unfortunately, lack of discipline crept into our game. R. Purdy was shown to the line following a late tackle. An 'outside the box' penalty decision lead to the Hoops pulling one back, and two further controversial goals followed, both involving deliberate interference with our keeper, T. Bantam. An onfield dispute after the second goal led to further red cards for two of our players and Manager Davie Ledley, who has resigned from his post following the incident.

This game, otherwise played in a sporting spirit by two young and talented teams, was marred by what many felt to be the over-reaction of the match official. I have every sympathy with the three lads concerned, who have a right to expect fair treatment from all involved in the game.

Regular readers of the First Team programme will be aware of the role Davie Ledley has played in promoting the Colts' side and I am sure all you 'Warneys' will join me in thanking him for his work in bringing our present Colts team into being.

Tommy Cowans
(Team Manager, Warne Colts)

TODAY'S TEAMS

WARNE COUNTY COLTS (Black & white stripes, black shorts)	v.	Wolverton (Old gold, black shorts)
Scott 1 Brocken 2 Small 3 Brown 4 Fish 5 McCall 6 Jezz 7 Mole 8 Matthews 9 Alexiou 10 Singh 11 Sub: McCann 12 UNAVAILABLE AT TIME OF GOING TO PRESS		Hamilton 1 Oganu 4 Quinn 3 Walter 5 Donau 6 Midnay 7 Dozzell 8 Wright 10 Lever 9 Morton 11 Simms 12 Priday 2 Malcolm 14

Match Officials

Ref: H. Thomas. Linesmen: A. Clint, E. Wyth

BRONTLEY LEAGUE

WESTERN AREA QUALIFYING COMPETITION

First Series Results

Hume United Colts	3	Warne County Colts	3
Olympic YC	3	Wolverton	1
Swanley	1	Queenstown	0

Second Series Fixtures

Warne County Colts	v.	Wolverton
Hume United Colts	v.	Queenstown
Olympic YC	v.	Swanley

League Table	P	W	D	L	F	A	Pts
Olympic YC	1	1	0	0	3	1	3
Swanley	1	1	0	0	1	0	3
Hume United Colts	1	0	1	0	3	3	1
Warne County Colts	1	0	1	0	3	3	1
Queenstown	1	0	0	1	0	1	0
Wolverton	1	0	0	1	1	3	0

WARNE COUNTY COLTS APPEARANCES AND GOAL-SCORERS
Bantam 1, Robinson 1, Alexiou 1, Mole 1, McCall 1, Purdy 1, McCann 1, Matthews 1, Jezz 1, Singh 1(2), Brocken 1, Fish 1s.
Opponents: OG 1.

TODAY'S MATCH:

WE WELCOME WOLVERTON FOR TODAY'S FIXTURE

Because of last Saturday's events Colts are forced to field an under-strength team, but we hope to include several new signings. Last week's draw with Hume was encouraging, and Colts can be expected to go all out to notch up our first win. Both sides are still feeling their way in this new competition, but a close-fought match appears likely.

Manager Cowan's assessment is that we need to average two points a game to be sure of qualification for the Premier Division of the Brontley League, which commences next season, so a win today would put us on course for that target. Our opponents are also in need of points, after losing their opening game to Olympic YC, who could turn out to be the surprise package of the competition. May the best team win ... so long as it is Warne County!

NEXT WEDNESDAY AT THE LANE!

WALSINGHAM FLOODLIT CUP (Semifinal) 2nd Leg

WARNE COUNTY v. CARLSCROFT UNITED
(1st leg 1–3) KO 7.30 p.m.

4. Warne County Colts v. Wolverton

This is the team line-up for our Second Series game against Wolverton in the Brontley League Western Area Qualifying Competition:

Scott
Brocken Small Alexiou McCall
Brown Fish
Jezz Matthews Mole Singh
Sub: McCann

I was really choked.

It was our first home game, so a whole lot of the Red Row kids had turned up to see me scoring Napper Super Goals and I was left sitting on the bench in my track suit. It wasn't even as if Tommy had changed the team and opted to play defensively. He hadn't. He had kept Joe Fish in the side, with orders to go forward when he could, which is what Joe likes doing best, but it meant that the back five we had played with under Davie Ledley became a back four under Tommy. We were playing with two attacking midfielders because Harpur would go forward much more than Ronnie was allowed to. We had an extra man up front as a striker, where Danny was back and Jezz had been switched out to the right.

Tommy told us it was the way he wanted us to play in future, because it would suit our players better.

'Five at the back must have been Davie Ledley's idea,' Jezz said to me, and I thought he was right. The switch to four at the front was a good sign for both of us, but it was better for Jezz than it was for me, because he was the one picked to go wide outside.

'Wish they'd put Danny wide, and left me in the middle,' Jezz said.

'Wish I was playing!' I said.

It was funny, talking to Jezz, because we should have been big rivals, going for the same spot in the team, the extra striker, but somehow we seemed to end up talking about things together. Probably it was because neither of us was sure of a place in the team, and the other strikers were.

I suppose the big difference between the Wolverton game and the Hume game as far as we two were concerned was that it was the wide-on-the-right spot we were competing for now, not the role of playing in behind the two strikers.

Joe Fish had leap-frogged over us into that spot. It was probably a good decision, because Joe can defend as well as attack, and I hadn't showed much when we were defending against Hume.

Tommy talked to us before the game. He introduced Cyril and Harpur, and told us that Cyril was in the team to tighten things up at the back, and Harpur was in the team to create opportunities for the front-runners. He said they were in on our Chief Scout's recommendation, which was good enough for him.

He had hinted at training on Wednesday that we might start the match on Saturday playing 4–2–4, without saying who would be in the team, because I suppose he didn't know then if Cyril and Harpur would sign. He might have had to sign someone else, like Singhy's friend Hasty, and then the formation could have been different. The idea was that we were the home team and we were going to go at them. If it didn't work, and we had to defend, we would revert to 4–3–3 or 4–4–2. He said we'd spent too long in the Hume game defending, and part of the reason for that was that the midfielders went back, and the forwards were left isolated. Harpur had been brought in to fix that, and Joe was to play alongside Harpur in a two-man midfield, with Jezz going wide to give us balance. He said that Jezz filling in on the right would mean that Tom Brocken wouldn't have to make so many runs on that side and would be able to concentrate on defence, and that the introduction of Harpur behind Jezz would more than compensate for Tom holding back. He told Nicky McCall that he was expected to stay back this time. Nicky looked grumpy, but he had never got forward at all against Hume, when he was supposed to come up from the back, so really he had nothing to be grumpy about.

'Any questions?' Tommy asked.

'Who is doing the ball-winning midfield, Tommy?' Tom Brocken asked. Tommy had made it clear that Harpur was in the team to create things, not stop the other team, and Tom knew that Joe Fish wasn't really a ball-winner either.

'Next week's answer to that question is Ronnie, when he comes back after suspension,' Tommy said. 'This week, you'll have to work it out as you go along. I'll expect you and Alex and our new recruit, Smally here, to do what you can, and Joe can show us a new side to his talents, if he has to pull back.'

Cyril looked really chuffed!

Then Harpur put his hand up and said he normally played on the left of midfield, not the right.

Tommy said he and Joe could switch.

We went out.

I settled in the dug-out, after the kick-in.

'You'll get a run, son,' was all Tommy said to me, which didn't tell me a lot that I didn't know. I was hoping that if I did get in it would be in the central striking role, instead of Danny or Big Matty, and not out wide on the right, which isn't my natural game. I fancied playing in the centre, and moving on to Harpur's through balls. Harpur makes the players in front of him look good, when he is on his game . . . which he usually is. I thought he might have difficulties against Wolverton because of coming into a team for the first time. The four front men weren't used to the sort of service Harpur can provide, and they might make him look silly, as if he was giving the ball away, because they failed to spot what he was doing.

Another reason why I should have been on the team at the start! I know the way Harpur plays. I would have been able to link up with him and get a hat trick or something and then we would both have been sure of our places. As it was, with Ronnie Purdy and Robbo coming back, somebody was going to be dropped, and it might be Harpur.

If Harpur's chances didn't look good, what about mine? I wasn't even on the field, so how could I play myself into the team?

There was a fierce wind blowing, with some rain in it, and we lost the toss, which gave

Wolverton choice of ends. They decided to play with the wind.

We kicked off, but we couldn't get our passes together, and they moved into the attack. They weren't much from a ball-playing point of view, but they had four strong players strung across the centre of the park, Donau, Midnay, Dozzell and Wright, who simply ballooned the ball forward, every time they got it, to the two big strikers, Lever and Morton. Alex took Lever, and Cyril was on Morton.

The first three big boots were all to Morton, and Cyril cut them out without losing any sweat. Then Lever had a run down the right, and Alex timed his tackle perfectly and pushed the ball into touch. The throw went to Wright, moving up from the back, and Cyril went across, coming off his man, but Wright missed the opportunity to play the ball through and simply ballooned it into our area, where Ally Scott came off his line and made a confident catch. I was pleased for Ally, because he knew he was second-choice keeper, only in the side because of Tony's suspension, and he must have been worried by the wind.

Harpur got the ball, and played it inside the back, for Singhy to run on to. Singhy got it across, but their Number 5 cut it out. Another balloon down the middle from Donau. Cyril took it on his chest and played it to Joe, and

Joe put Singhy away. He went outside his man, then inside, and curled the ball back for Jezz, who was unmarked on the edge of the area.

Bang!

1–0 to us!

They came back at us with more big dolly drops and Ally was nearly caught out by one at the near post. The ball skidded off Ally's fingers and hit the post, but Tom Brocken managed to clear it off the line, and the corner came to nothing.

Another through ball from Harpur, and Big Matty got clear.

2–0 to us!

Then it was 3–0.

Jezz got it. He had wandered inside and he caught Donau in two minds and nipped it off his foot, then he hit a rising shot from about twenty metres into the top of the goal. It was a real rocket, a goal all the way!

We were on our way! Everybody was shouting and roaring!

Our strikers were ripping their defence apart. Jezz had two goals already and Matty had one and Danny Mole was chasing everything and going wild to get his name on the score-sheet as well.

And there I was, Red Row's Demon Goalscorer, sitting on the bench without even getting a chance to kick the ball!

We got a corner on the right and Singhy worked a short one with Nicky McCall. Nicky put in a centre, but their keeper came out and missed because the wind curled it away from him and it hit their right back and ballooned into the net, when really it was going nowhere.

4–0, and only about twenty minutes gone! Then it wasn't 4–0, because the ref ruled that Singhy had run offside.

'Is he ever onside?' Tommy muttered. I knew what he meant. The problem was that Singhy is so fast that he gets away from the defence easily, and if his runs aren't timed exactly right he gets offside. Even when he does time his run correctly, refs and linesmen often don't read it, because they can't believe anybody could have got there so fast from an onside position. Singhy was profiting most of all from Harpur's through balls, but wasting a lot of chances as well.

'Some player, your mate Harpur!' Tommy purred to me.

'Yes,' I said. 'We used to link up a lot, down at Red Row. He made a lot of goals for me.'

Tommy didn't take the hint. He was so intent on following the game that I don't think he even knew it was a hint!

Wolverton were right out of it. They weren't bad players, but when they did get possession they had no one who could use it.

'Combination's all wrong,' Tommy said to Mr Hope. 'It's all hump the ball upfield and chase it. What they need is one or two players to stop the ball, and take a look at what is going on. Their big lads can play a bit, but at the moment they are chasing around after nothing.'

It was making Cyril Small and Alex look good, because they were lying off the two strikers and the balls that were coming through were easy to read and intercept. The high balls, which should have been a problem, tended to be over-hit and carry through to the keeper. Partly that was because of the wind, but the real problem was a lack of accuracy. If the balls had been better placed, Cyril and Alex would have had to tighten up on their men, and then the advantage in height and weight would have been against them.

'They're giving us a cosy ride at the back!' Tommy said, and I think that that just about summed it up. Most of the play was at the front, anyway, with our Colts streaming forward even though the wind was right against them.

Everybody started getting in on the act. Harpur had a long drive deflected for a corner and Nicky McCall had another saved by the keeper at the foot of the post and then Nicky had another go, a header that hit the bar and went over, when he should have scored because Matty had put him clear.

'I told Nicky to stay back!' Tommy said with a grin. 'Last week, when I told him to get up, he never moved. Now he thinks he's a centre-forward!'

Then we got a penalty, when Nicky was pulled down from behind by their Number 3, Quinn.

Tom Brocken took it, but the goalie parried his shot, and the ball broke out to Jezz, who tapped it into the back of the net for his hat trick.

4–0, after thirty-eight minutes.

Our fans were going wild! There weren't that many of them, all huddled under cover out of the wind and the rain, but they cheered us like mad.

We kept attacking, and Wolverton were forced right back and hardly got out of their half, but the ball just wouldn't go in the net.

4–0 at half-time.

I thought I was bound to get on for the second half, and with any luck I'd get on the score-sheet. He wasn't going to take Jezz off when Jezz was going mad and running all over the defence getting hat tricks, but I thought I might get on for Danny Mole, who hadn't done a lot, or Matty.

Tommy didn't say much in the dressing-room. 'Don't go mad. Don't lose your shape!' Stuff like that.

Then Mr Hope called him over to look at Alex. Somebody had taken a kick at him, and Alex's right leg was a mess.

'Thought you'd disappeared a bit, towards the end,' Tommy said. 'That looks as if it needs a stitch!'

Then he told me to warm up.

Alex was mad. He didn't want to come off, but his leg was all bloody, and Mr Hope told him to hop in the shower and clean himself up, and then they would go down to the hospital.

'No need to,' Tommy said, over his shoulder. 'Club Doc is up in the stand. He'll see to the lad.'

So I was on.

I thought Tommy was going to put me on in a straight swap for Alex, which would have put me in the centre of the defence, helping Cyril, but he didn't.

'Try doing what you didn't manage last week, son,' he said, and he switched Joe Fish back into the centre of the defence, and put me alongside Harpur, but on the right this time, not the left. I was tucked in behind the strikers again, only this time the strikers would be going forward to add to the goals we'd already got.

'Careful!' Tommy said. 'Remember last week. Three goals up and you blew it.'

The way we started the second half, I don't

think anybody had paid any attention to Tommy. We had the wind behind us and it was swirling and gusting right into their goal. We thought we might score about twenty, but it didn't work out like that.

Mostly it was the wind. Playing against it, the ball had held up and Jezz and Lester Singh had been able to get it over, and it had hung in the air so that Danny and Big Matty could get on the end of crosses, but when we tried it in the second half, the wind just blew the ball out for goal-kicks, or carried it too close to the keeper.

Their keeper had made a few mistakes in the first half, but he made up for it in the second. He kept coming off his line fast, and with the wind making the ball over-carry he had a lot of it to do. He took the ball from Matty twice when Matty was clean through, and then he tackled Jezz outside the area and screwed the ball into touch. That was a missed chance, because Jezz could have turned it inside to me, but he had already scored three and wasn't thinking about anything else. He booted it past the back and went haring for the goal again, but the ball overran because of the wind, and it was easy pickings for the keeper.

I was trying to get forward, because there wasn't anything to do at the back, but the problem was that everybody else was doing it too. Then I nearly mucked things up, moving on to a through ball from Harpur after I'd sprinted out of defence. Their Number 4 got the ball from me and laid it forward into the space where I should have been, and they got away and would have scored if Ally hadn't stuck out a leg and deflected the ball for a corner.

Tommy was up out of the dug-out yelling at me.

The trouble was that Tom Brocken had given up being a defender and kept steaming forward on my right, and Nicky McCall was doing the same thing on my left and I was left as third man at the back, with Joe and Cyril, picking up the ball whenever Wolverton managed to get it forward, which wasn't often. Harpur had wandered so far upfield that I couldn't link with him and I was left not knowing what I should do. Nicky or Tom should have been doing it but weren't. Nicky was upfield all the time, and Tom had so much room that it wasn't true, with nobody coming at him at all. I couldn't blame him for going forward. I would have!

Then Nicky got a goal, running on to a pass from Harpur that split their defence completely.

Nicky should never have been left clear, because they should have got back, but their sub, Malcolm, who should have covered him, was caught badly out of position, and Nicky drove it in by the near post. Jezz had gone into the centre trying to poach another, and really he was offside, but the ref didn't spot him. Even if he wasn't, Tom Brocken was, which shows the way things were going, with two of our back players charging through in the attack!

On a day when we weren't 5–0 up, the ref *would* have spotted Tom offside, but when it didn't matter at all, he didn't.

5–0 to County!

Then they brought their second sub on after Oganu was hurt. Their Number 12, Simms, was small, but he and the other sub, Malcolm, could both use the ball, and Wolverton began to come back into the game. They started laying on decent balls for the strikers, which gave Cyril a chance to pull out one or two of his famous slide-tackles. Altogether Wolverton looked much better, but it was too late.

We were still well in control.

Jezz, who was all over the place having got his hat trick, turned up on the left of the area, took the ball clean off Singhy's foot, and banged it against the foot of the post, when he could have played it inside to Nicky, who was clear and unmarked.

'My ball!' Nicky yelled, looking disgusted.

Jezz just grinned.

I don't think he fancied the idea of a striker

giving up a shot at goal to pass to a defender who'd wandered upfield out of position.

5–0 was the final score.

Cyril jumped about at the final whistle as if we had won the FA Cup!

'You killed us!' their Number 8 said, coming across to me as we were walking off. 'Thought you were supposed to be a bunch of hackers?'

'Eh?' I said.

'Three men sent off against Hume!' he said. 'Our Manager pulled all the playmakers out of the team and put the muscle in, and the only one who got kicked was your Number 10.'

He meant Alexiou.

The County Chairman, Mr Murphy, who makes the crisps, was down in the corridor clapping everybody on the back and saying what a wonderful game it was.

We got into the dressing-room, and Tommy came in.

'Call yourselves footballers?' he said.

He didn't say anything more.

He just stood there glaring at us.

Then he stomped out.

There was dead silence.

'5–0!' somebody said.

'We were brilliant!' Cyril Small said. 'Ey-a-adoo! We're going top of the league!'

Then we all started singing 'We are the

Champions', because you can't do much better than 5–0 and we reckoned if we could win 5–0 against a team that only lost 3–1 the week before, we were about two goals better than the team that beat them, Olympic. Olympic were top of the table after the first series, so we had to be in with a shout!

'That was a cakewalk!' Cyril said to me after we'd changed. 'If they are all like that we ought to walk it into this Premier Division thingy.'

'Rotten game, though,' Harper said. 'They didn't come into it until the subs came on, and then it was too late. Those two should have been on from the start, and it might have been closer. We weren't much cop either. Everybody was playing for himself.'

'5–0!' Cyril shouted. 'Man. United here I come!'

Harpur was right, as usual. Everybody in the team knew that we had three players coming back from suspension who were certain to be in the side, and that meant three players would have to drop out. One of them would be Ally Scott, who had had nothing much to do anyway, but the other two places were up for grabs.

I didn't say anything. Judging by the way Tommy had picked the team so far, I knew who the first player left out would be. Harpur and Cyril would be all right. Neither of them had put a foot wrong. No goals against, not even a half-chance that they could be blamed for. But I was supposed to come on to do the Supersub act, scoring goals by picking off balls from the two strikers, and I had ended up making up the number at the back while the so-called defenders like Tom Brocken and Nicky McCall waltzed off to score goals and . . . and . . .

Jezz got a hat trick!

Not me . . . *Jezz*.

Tommy wouldn't drop Matty or Danny Mole, so it had to be me or Jezz. Jezz was our top scorer with four goals in two games, if you counted the OG the back scored when we played Hume, and three in two games, plus an assist, if you didn't count it as a goal. Scoring goals is what strikers *do*, and I hadn't been doing it, which meant I was O-U-T.

P-r-o-b-a-b-l-y.

Maybe not. Jezz had hogged the ball and wasted a lot of chances running all over the place and not passing, and I'd done piles of covering when our defenders went mad, which was what I had to do, because there was no one else to do it. The thing was, Wolverton hardly got out of their own penalty area until they changed their team around late on, so nobody had a chance to spot what I was doing, covering at the back.

Maybe Tommy had noticed it.

It is a Manager's job to spot things like that.

It was also our Manager's job to make sure we qualified for the Premier Division by finishing in the top three in the Qualifying Competition and, with a win and a draw behind us, I didn't reckon he was going to experiment by changing his strikers. Cyril and Harpur would keep their places in the team, and so would Joe Fish . . . all my mates from Red Row Stars v. St Gabriel's, and I would be the one left sitting with Ally Scott on the subs' bench.

Except that it wouldn't be Ally. With fifteen players to choose from for the next game, Ally would be up in the stand, and two outfield players would be on the bench.

Which two?

5. Show-down with the Manager

Monday was bad at school.

Dribbler and Daniel and some of the others had been down to the game, and they had spread the word that I didn't do much. They were saying how unlucky I was being made sub, and how I hadn't had much chance when I did get on. All I could do was agree with them.

'Serve you right for being a Big-head and boasting about your football!' Ugly Irma said.

She went on about it so much that even our Avril was fed up. She told Ugly Irma to go and take a running jump, and they would have had a row about it if Miss Fellows hadn't butted in and stopped them.

I was down in the dumps.

Then, on Wednesday when we went down to Owen Lane for training, it was even worse.

There were two new players, Viney and Smart. Somebody had recommended them to Tommy for our Squad. That made sixteen players altogether, and my chances of making the team looked even worse.

Then Tommy read out the sheet for our away game against Olympic YC and I wasn't on it. I wasn't even in the subs. Tommy said he wanted to see Nicky McCall, Ally Scott and me in his office after training, and we weren't to slope off without talking to him.

'What's that about?' Cyril asked me.

'Don't know,' I said, but I thought I did. Tommy had said from the start that he didn't want too big a Squad because we had no reserve team, and it wasn't fair to keep players on the club's books when they had no chance of a game. He had brought in four new players in two weeks, Cyril and Harpur from the old Red Row team and the two new ones that nobody knew anything about, and that meant that somebody had to be shown the dressing-room door.

That is what Ally and I thought it was, anyway. Ally already knew he was only in as cover for Tony Bantam. We thought Tommy might decide to let him go. I had played in two games without making any impression, and that made me another candidate for the high jump.

Nicky didn't say anything to either of us when we went down to wait in the First Team billiard room outside Tommy's office.

Nicky went in first.

He was in about ten minutes, and when he

came out he didn't even say one word. His eyes were shiny and his face was flushed, as if he was going to burst into tears.

'Napper?' Tommy called.

'Good luck!' Ally said.

I went into the office.

'Have a seat, son,' Tommy said.

I sat down.

I'd only been in the office once before, and that was when Davie Ledley signed me on. Two trips, one to sign on, the other to sign off. The only good thing about it was that I'd be able to stop writing my Football Career Book for Miss Fellows if I was chucked out, because I wouldn't have a decent team to play for. The bad thing was that I wouldn't have a football career.

'You're not in the team,' he said. 'Not even on the bench. That doesn't feel good, does it?'

I nodded. He'd been a player; he knew what if felt like. That is what he was saying to me. Except that he had been a *real* player, a Scottish International. He'd *had* his football career, that was the big difference. It didn't look as if mine was going to last much longer.

Then he said something that really floored me.

'I'm not going to name names, Napper,' Tommy said, 'but there are four or five players in the Squad who have the potential to make something of themselves as footballers, and you are one of them.'

'Then . . . then why am I not in the team?' I burst out. If I was so good I had to be in the team, as far as I could see.

'Because having potential isn't the same thing as doing it for me out on the park,' he said. 'I have a job to do, short-term, and that is to make sure we start the Brontley League in the Premier Division. Right? When we do, I'd lay odds that you'll be part of it. But – and it is a big but – you haven't been doing it so far, and I have three games coming up where I have to get the right results.'

'Yes,' I said.

'I don't want you walking out on me because you are not playing,' he said. 'Is that clear? That's why I've called you in here, because I know the way you must be feeling. But the bottom line is that I'm chancing things by playing four strikers as it is. Jezz I can't leave out because he is getting goals, Singhy gives me width on the left, Matty is a real work-horse, and Danny Mole shows every sign of coming good. So what do I do? How do I put you in?'

'I can read Harpur Brown's game,' I said. 'I've played with him trillions of times, when I was main striker.'

'You want in on Harpur's back?' he said. 'He's supposed to carry you because you have a good understanding?'

Put that way, it sounded bad.

'I need a result this week!' he said. 'We get one, and we should be home and dry. Then I can afford to experiment and give you a run, somehow. Maybe I'll rest Danny, or the big fellow, and give you a go down the middle, where you want to play.'

He seemed to think I was going to say something, but I couldn't think of anything sensible, so I just sat there looking at him.

'You're younger than most of the Squad, Napper. You drift in and out of the game. Sometimes, like last week, I don't see you at all. That's not unusual, with young players.'

'Last week wasn't my fault,' I said. 'All the defenders were attacking. It was stupid. Somebody had to hang back, or Cyril and Joe could have been in trouble.'

He nodded.

'So I wasn't out of the game,' I said. 'I wasn't out of it, because I was covering for other people. If I'd gone up they could have caught us at the back.'

'I did notice,' he said. 'That's why I am bothering about you now. You and your mate Harpur can both read the game, and adjust your patterns of play to fit in with the others. That is something that nobody can teach you. You either have it, or you haven't. But it isn't enough to be able to read the game, you have to play a bit too, turn on something extra special when it is needed. Harpur did last week, you didn't. He's in, you are out. For now. But stay around. We may need you.'

Long silence. I wasn't sure that *maybe* being needed was good enough. Star players aren't maybes, they are the first names down on the sheet!

'OK, son?' he said.

'OK,' I said. 'I suppose so.'

'See you Saturday!' he said. 'Don't lose heart. You're a good footballer!'

Then I got up to go.

'Remember to bring your boots!' Tommy shouted after me.

What for? I thought, but I didn't say it. My boots wouldn't do me much good, sitting in the stand.

Ally went in, giving me a nervous grin as I passed him.

I had to wait for Mr Hope to get my lift home in his car, and Cyril was waiting too, because Mr Hope drops him off on the way. It was part of the arrangement made with Cyril's dad, when Mr Hope and George Trotman were trying to talk him into letting Cyril sign for County.

Cyril had gone out to the running track by the tunnel entrance. He was standing looking at the ground.

It was dark. They didn't put the floodlights on for our training, just the lights in the stand. The pitch was all shadowy, what we could see of it. It was easy to imagine being out there playing for County, scoring hat tricks, with the big lights on and a crowd in the ground.

'Brilliant, isn't it?' Cyril said. 'Us . . . in a big team!'

'Yes,' I said. 'I suppose so.'

Cyril must have noticed the odd note in my voice.

'He's not letting you go, is he?' he said.

'Don't think so,' I said. 'Not now, anyway. He just wanted to talk about not putting me in the team.'

'You'll get in it,' Cyril said. 'You were the best player in the Stars.'

'After Harpur,' I said.

'Yeah, well. Harpur is special,' he said. Then he repeated: 'You'll get in the team. You've got to get in the team. He can't go on leaving you out.'

'Tell that to Tommy,' I said.

That was it.

We went back down the tunnel.

Nicky McCall was coming out of the dressing-room. He looked surprised to see us. I suppose he thought everyone had gone home.

'OK, Nicky?' Cyril said.

'Oh yes, fine!' he said. 'Chucked me out of

the Squad, didn't he? It looks as if I went to the wrong school!'

We didn't know what he meant.

'My face doesn't fit, does it?' he said. 'You don't get to stay on here unless your face fits. This place is filling up with players from one mucky little kids' team, from a school whose Headmaster just happens to be palsy-walsy with George Trotman!'

We just stared at him.

'I hope you get beat, Saturday!' he said, and off he went.

The dressing-room door was lying open.

We looked inside.

Everything was upside-down.

'Better clear it up, or there'll be trouble,' I said.

So we did.

We got the kit back in the hamper, more or less, and the words off the walls.

'McCall's an idiot,' Cyril said. 'You know what he meant about one mucky little school, don't you?'

'Yes,' I said. 'Red Row!'

'It isn't true, anyway,' Cyril said. 'There are only three of us, four if you count Joe Fish, although he didn't play for us. I suppose he wouldn't have been in the team without Mr Hope's say-so though.'

'Three,' I said. 'I'm not in the team either.'

'Nicky's a doughnut!' Cyril said.

It was true. Tell Nicky to lie back, and he'd move up. Tell him to go forward, and he'd lie back. Nicky didn't have any idea about playing to a pattern, but I still felt sorry for him.

It was easier for me to understand than it was for Cyril.

Cyril was in the team, and I wasn't.

So I could understand what Nicky must have been feeling after Tommy Cowans showed him the door.

All I could do was to turn up Saturday . . . with my boots, just in case . . . and hope something would happen to get me back on to the team.

Olympic Youth Club

Olympic YC v. Warne County Colts

Teams:

OLYMPIC YOUTH CLUB (Red)		**Warne County Colts** (Black & white stripes)
From:		From:
Hilley	1	Bantam
Once	2	Brocken
Dyall	3	Small
Hilton	4	Fish
Rolston	5	Robinson
Indont	6	Purdy
Lamont	7	Brown
Taylor	8	Mole
Dola	9	Matthews
Straw	10	Jezz
Claymore	11	Singh
Richardson	12	Smart
Dooley	14	Alexiou

Match Officials:
Ref: B. Raymond. Linesmen: H. Orr, P. Patmore

Last week's results

Warne County Colts	5	Wolverton	0
Hume Colts	1	Queenstown	1
Olympic YC	4	Swanley	2

League Table	**P**	**W**	**D**	**L**	**F**	**A**	**Pts**
Olympic YC	2	2	0	0	7	3	6
Warne County Colts	2	1	1	0	8	3	4
Swanley	2	1	0	1	3	4	3
Hume Colts	2	0	2	0	4	4	2
Queenstown	2	0	1	1	1	2	1
Wolverton	2	0	0	2	1	8	0

PRODUCTION OF THIS PROGRAMME SPONSORED BY
THE BRONTLEY BUILDING SOCIETY

6. Olympic YC v. Warne County Colts

This is the team that lined up for our third match in the Brontley League Western Area Qualifying Competition, away to Olympic YC:

Bantam
Brocken Small Fish Robinson
Purdy Brown
Jezz Matthews Smart Singh
Subs: Alexiou, Mole

It wasn't the team that Tommy had read out to us after training on Wednesday night. We didn't know there was going to be any change until we were on the coach going to Stadney, where Olympic YC played their games. Tommy sat with Danny Mole and talked to him for about ten minutes. Danny didn't look too pleased, but it wasn't until we were in the dressing-room at Stadney that Tommy announced the change.

The new guy, Smart, was in, leading the line, and Danny was on the bench.

Danny wasn't the only one who felt choked. I was too. Tommy had taken a long time telling me he couldn't leave one of his strikers out and then, the first time a new striker came along, he was in the team.

I was really glad to get out of the dressing-room, because I didn't want anybody to see how mad I was. Stuck in the stand, not even on the bench!

Except that there wasn't a stand, just a tin hut by the changing-rooms, with a few chairs in it. It wasn't even a proper ground. There was no terrace, just a field with a fence round it, and the field didn't belong to Olympic YC. They only had the use of it so they could get their names in for the Brontley League Premier. It was one of the rules of the League, that competing clubs had to have fully enclosed grounds with proper facilities. That was no problem for us or Hume United Colts or Wolverton or any of the established clubs, but it was for Olympic YC.

We thought Olympic were a hick outfit. They hadn't a decent ground of their own and they couldn't manage a proper programme either. All they had was a sheet with the players' names on it, and a list of results and the league table.

I thought I wouldn't stick it in my Football Career Book because it wasn't a proper programme and I wasn't in the team.

'How come this lot are top of the table?' Ally asked me as we were waiting for the teams to come out.

'Because *we* haven't played them yet!' I said. They wouldn't be top of the table when we beat them. We should have won against Hume if the ref hadn't gone mad, and we proved we could play against Wolverton, so nobody really believed we had anything to fear against a Youth Club team.

The Western Area was looking good for us because we had beaten Wolverton 5–0 and Olympic could only manage 3–1, so we thought we could handle them without much bother. They had won their game against Swanley 4–2, and we had drawn ours 3–3 with Hume. That meant they were on six points and we were on four, but we had the advantage on goal difference, plus five against plus four. Ally and I weren't certain if goal difference counted in the Qualifiers, but we thought it probably did. If we beat them, goal difference wouldn't matter anyway because we would go top of the table with seven points and they would be stuck on six. The next two teams were Swanley, who had three points, and Hume, who had two, but they were playing each other, so one of them was bound to drop points. The other two were probably out of it already, stuck at the bottom of the table. We only had to finish in the top three to qualify for the Premier Division, so we looked like dead certs!

'I bet this team are rubbish!' Ally said to me. 'They aren't attached to one of the big clubs, and nobody would want to sign for them when he could be with a proper team!'

I thought he was probably right, but I didn't care much. We were both out of the team, that was what counted. Ally had been told right out that Tony was first choice. Tommy said he wanted Ally in the Squad, but it was up to Ally if he wanted to stay, knowing he wouldn't be in the team. If Tommy was going to muck me about the way he had, bringing Smart in from nowhere to take the main striking role down the middle when he wouldn't even give me a chance, he had another think coming. Maybe Ally would go with me, and we could find another club where we'd both get in the team.

Our new striker looked the part. He was big, with legs like tree trunks, and his hair slicked back. He spent the kick-in period practising volleys that he got the two subs to lay on for him, as if they were his personal servants or something.

'Tottenham are supposed to be after him,' Ally said. 'That's what I heard. Or Man. United. One of those. And he's supposed to be going to the FA School, so we are lucky to have him in our team.'

Some luck! I didn't think it was lucky, and I

was sure Danny Mole didn't think so either. He was sitting on the bench, but he kept well away from Tommy, with his head down.

I knew how Danny felt. We were both in the same boat.

'Let's see how he plays,' I said, and we settled back to watch Tommy's wonder-boy striker.

We didn't see much of him.

The match had hardly started when we were 1–0 down.

The goal was a penalty, when Harpur Brown handled inside the box. Harpur didn't mean to do it. He looked really disgusted with himself, although the ref didn't even caution him, which he could have done, for deliberate handball.

'If it wasn't deliberate, it couldn't be a penalty,' Ally said to me. 'And if it was deliberate in the box, he should have been off.'

Anyway, Harpur wasn't off, and it was a penalty, and Tony had no chance with the shot.

1–0 to Olympic.

It could have been much worse. Tony Bantam was playing a blinder, even though he didn't get near the spot-kick, and Cyril was tackling anything that moved. Ronnie Purdy was all over the place, threatening to get himself booked again and giving us all cold sweats. The problem was Tom Brocken and Robbo, the two wide backs. Their wide men were turning Tom and Robbo inside out, every time they got the ball. Jezz had pulled back to help Tom, but Singhy had his orders to stay up, and so Robbo was exposed. Harpur had to help him, which cut off the supply going forwards.

Not that we had much to go forwards to.

Smart, the wonder boy, didn't seem to think there was anybody else on the field. He didn't pass when he got the ball, and he didn't make runs for anybody else. He spent his time yelling at people to pass to him, and then yelling when the ball wasn't exactly spot on where he wanted it. Jezz and Matty were both doing their best, but nothing came from Smart at all.

Then he yelled once too often, at Ronnie Purdy. Ronnie had made one of his few runs forward, laying the ball off into Smart's path, and going for the return, which, of course, didn't come, because Smarty decided to juggle the ball round the back instead. He was flattened for his trouble, although Ronnie had got free, because their defence hadn't expected him to run on.

'My ball, Smarty!' Ronnie said, trotting past Smart as he lay on the ground.

Smart disentangled himself from the back, and then he got up and ran back into our half, after Ronnie. It was the first time he'd been in our half, because covering back definitely wasn't his game.

He came up to Ronnie, red-faced, and yelled something at him.

I don't know what it was.

The next moment they were down on the ground, scuffling with each other, with Tom Brocken sprinting across to part them and Tommy Cowans running on and the ref blowing away on his whistle like mad.

I thought they might both be sent off, but all they got was a lecture.

Tommy came off the field, and told Danny Mole to start warming up.

We thought it was just to give Smart something to think about, but it wasn't. Five minutes later Danny was on, and Smart was on his way into the changing-rooms, red-faced with anger. 'So far as I'm concerned Manchester United can have him!' Ally said.

The trouble was that our team had lost all its shape and rhythm, sorting the problem out. Olympic were firing on all cylinders and they got a second goal just before half-time, when Tony Bantam missed his punch at a corner and their centre-half nodded the ball back over him into the net.

It was a well-taken goal and we couldn't really blame Tony, because he had been under pressure for most of the half, and it was the first mistake he had made.

Half-time: Olympic YC 2 – Warne County Colts 0!

'It could have been five!' Ally said to me, and he was spot on.

The game had got right away from us. It wasn't that they were so great. We hadn't got going at all. Maybe it was the upset over Smarty mucking everybody about, or maybe it was that we'd reckoned they were a soft touch . . . which wasn't very clever, considering they were top of the table, and unbeaten. I suppose we'd all convinced ourselves that they must be a 'nothing' team because they were just a Youth Club without a proper ground or a programme or a stand. The reality was that they'd been playing together as a team in the Northern Bell League all season, and our team was still made up of individual players who hadn't had time to settle in together.

'We're as good as they are, we're just not putting it together,' Ally said to me.

I don't know what Tommy said to our team in the dressing-room, because we weren't playing, and we didn't think we were supposed to go in, though Tommy said afterwards that we should have, because he wanted everyone to know what was happening when it came to team talks.

When the teams came out for the second half, Alex had been brought in for Joe Fish, to stiffen the defence. He was so keen to show Tommy he could do it that he was booked for almost the first tackle he made, and then he was afraid of being sent off and hardly tackled at all. The result was that the man he was marking got away and drew Tony from his line and chipped him.

3–0 to Olympic.

Then Alex really panicked, and scythe-tackled his man the next time he got the ball. The ref didn't spot it, but Tommy did, and was up out of the dug-out shouting to Alex to cool down. We didn't want to risk having another player sent off, because there had been a row after the Hume game. It wasn't about the sendings-off, although they were what caused it. The row was about what Tommy had written in our programme for the game with Wolverton when he said he had every sympathy with the lads who were sent off, because they didn't get fair treatment from the ref. It was something like that. The Brontley League Foundation Committee wrote a stinker of a letter to the Warne County Chairman, D. Murphy. The club was warned about its future conduct. There was also something about 'standards of behaviour on and off the field' being taken into consideration when the Premier Division places were decided. That worried everybody. We didn't want to win our place in the Premier and then be ruled out of it because we had a bad disciplinary record.

That was why Tommy was so busy yelling at Alex to cool it, and probably why he was so upset about Ronnie and his wild tackles, not to mention the fight on the field with Smarty-pants.

We were still 0–3 down, whether or not our disciplinary record was at risk, and things didn't get any better as the second half went on.

When we had the ball, which wasn't often, nothing much was happening up front. Harpur played some good balls through, mainly to Jezz, but Jezz didn't read them at all. He wanted the ball to his feet all the time, so that he could draw his man on, and he didn't seem to realize that that wasn't working. Four times he was dumped, losing possession, and then he didn't fancy it, and began to wander inside. Tommy spotted it, and he signalled Matty to move out wide. Matty picked up the next two balls from Harpur and got to the byline, but when the ball came over Jezz couldn't get on the end of it.

Right at the end, Singhy got away on his own and managed to nick one back, with a ball that crashed against the under-side of the bar and came down goal-side of the line, although the Olympic players said it didn't. They were shouting at the ref, but he didn't send anybody off for it.

We should have had him reffing the game against Hume!

Olympic YC 3–Warne Colts 1.

'Nicky McCall might have made a difference,' Ally said to me, when we were waiting in the coach for the others. 'Alex had a really poor game.'

'Nicky played the way *he* wanted to,' I said. 'When he was supposed to attack against Hume, he didn't, and when Tommy told him to concentrate on defence against Wolverton he spent the game in their penalty area, trying to score so that he would look good.'

'So did everybody else,' Ally said.

'I didn't,' I said. 'Didn't stop me being taken off the bench this time, though.'

'Me too,' Ally said. The difference was that he hadn't really expected to hold his place against Tony Bantam, and I had been replaced in our thirteen by Smarty-pants.

Tommy didn't say a word to me about it on the coach, but Mr Hope did in the car, after we left Owen Lane to drive home.

'What is the long face about, Napper?' he said. 'Upset because you weren't in the team?'

I told him it wasn't that. It was Tommy telling me one minute that he couldn't drop his strikers to fit me in, and bringing in Smarty-pants for the very next game, in my position.

Mr Hope shrugged.

'That is the way it goes, Napper,' he said. 'The boy was recommended to us. He showed up. Tommy didn't intend to play him, but then we got word that one or two of the League clubs had come calling at his door. George Trotman had Tommy in and told him to play the boy, so we could see what he was made of. Tommy was only doing what he was told.'

'Y-e-s,' I said.

'We won't be seeing Mr Smart again!' Mr Hope said. 'You have nothing to worry about there. Or young Viney either. He took a look round the place on Wednesday, and cleared off. They both think they are First Division material . . . which is more than anybody else does.'

'Maybe *we* are!' Cyril piped up from the back. Cyril always thinks big.

'Well, if you are, Tommy is as good a Coach as you'll find, Cyril.' Mr Hope said. Then he said something about the really big clubs like Man. United and Spurs and Arsenal signing up too many kids too early, so that they got discouraged when they didn't make much progress to begin with.

'If either of you looks like making the grade, an outfit like County is the best place to be,' Mr Hope said. 'Big enough to know the job, but not so big that you get swamped out by crowds of schoolboy international players roped in from all over the country.'

That was all right, if you got in the team.

The way I saw it, I wasn't even getting a

look-in with County, so my chances of making it to one of the big clubs were nix!

'Be patient, Napper,' Mr Hope said. 'Tommy rates you. You'll get your chance, when people stop interfering with him and let him do his job.'

That was all right, in a way. George Trotman had made Tommy put Smarty-pants in the team, and Tommy hadn't wanted to do it. Tommy hadn't been going behind my back, and telling me lies so that I wouldn't walk out of the Squad.

That was just fine . . . except that I still wasn't in the team!

'Chin up, Napper,' Mr Hope said. 'Wait till next week. Maybe you'll get your chance then.'

Maybe . . . and maybe not!

'You going to stick it out if you're not in the team next week?' Cyril asked me when Mr Hope got out at the petrol station.

'I suppose so,' I said.

Tommy had told Nicky McCall that he wasn't good enough straight to his face. He had also let Reidy and Zan and Birdy go, because he knew they didn't fit in with his plans, so he wasn't afraid to face up to disappointing people by letting them go.

If he didn't want me in the Squad, he would have told me so.

Unless he didn't want to annoy Mr Hope.

Maybe I was only being kept on to keep Mr Hope happy, because he was the one who recommended me in the first place. That is what Nicky McCall had seemed to think was happening anyway.

I couldn't work it out for myself.

'I'll stick it out a bit longer,' I said.

I still thought I could make it with County, even if Tommy was picking Jezz instead of me.

All I needed was a chance to get in the team and score some goals.

OWEN LANE STADIUM

WARNE COUNTY COLTS

v.

SWANLEY

Brontley League: Western Area Qualifying Competition

KO 11 a.m.

PRODUCTION OF THIS PROGRAMME SPONSORED BY

THE BRONTLEY BUILDING SOCIETY

NOTES FROM OUR CHAIRMAN, Mr Duncan Murphy

Elsewhere we publish a statement issued on behalf of the club regarding certain comments by our Colts' Manager which appeared in the last issue of this programme. This statement is self-explanatory. The referee's job is not an easy one and it is important that we all recognize how difficult it can be. The decisions went against us, two vital points were lost, and no fewer than three of our players were dismissed for trivial offences. Tommy spoke out in defence of the young lads concerned. Perhaps he was wrong to do so. That is certainly the view taken by the Brontley League Foundation Committee. The matter is now closed.

Duncan Murphy

TOMMY SAYS...

Football is a funny game. You are up one week, and down the next. At least, that is the feeling at the Lane, where a 5–0 victory against Wolverton was followed by a surprise 3–1 defeat at the hands of Olympic YC. Performance to date has been erratic, as is only to be expected with a team still struggling to find its feet, but the signs for the future are encouraging.

In last week's game, keeper Tony Bantam was outstanding, as were Small and Purdy at the back. Brown did enough to suggest that he will be an asset for the future, once he settles into the team, but our forwards were disappointing. Our goal came from winger Lester Singh and was a cracker! Individually our front players did well, but they are still not playing for each other.

TOMMY

AN APOLOGY

WARNE COUNTY FC and Mr B. Simms

We have been asked to state that comments in the last issue were not intended as a criticism of the above official. It is the policy of the Brontley League Foundation Committee to discourage dissent on the field of play, and we accept that Mr Simms acted in accordance with this policy. We take this opportunity to apologize unreservedly to Mr Simms.

TODAY'S TEAMS

WARNE COUNTY COLTS (Black & white stripes, black shorts)	v.	**Swanley** (Blue shirts, white shorts)
~~Bantam~~ Scott 1	1	Orme 1
Brocken 2	2	Hatten 4
Small 4	3	Bridey 5
Fish 5	4	Dortland 2
Robinson 3	5	Maginn 3
Purdy 6	6	Wictck 10
Brown 7	7	Allen 6
Mole 8	8	Ritz 7
Matthews 9	9	Clemens 8
Jezz 10	10	Jones 9
Singh 11	11	Hamer 11
Alexiou 12	12	Bolby 12
McCann 14	14	Alouse 14

Match Officials

Ref: D. Jones. Linesmen: K. Koo, H. Partridge

BRONTLEY LEAGUE

WESTERN AREA QUALIFYING COMPETITION

Third Series Results

Olympic YC	3	Warne Colts	1
Swanley	0	Hume Colts	1
Queenstown	2	Wolverton	0

Fourth Series Fixtures

Warne Colts	v.	Swanley
Wolverton	v.	Hume Colts
Queenstown	v.	Olympic YC

League Table	P	W	D	L	F	A	Pts
Olympic YC	3	3	0	0	10	4	9
Hume Colts	3	1	2	0	5	4	5
Warne Colts	3	1	1	1	9	6	4
Queenstown	3	1	1	1	3	2	4
Swanley	3	1	0	2	3	5	3
Wolverton	3	0	0	3	1	10	0

WARNE COUNTY COLTS APPEARANCES AND GOAL-SCORERS
Bantam 2, Scot 1, Brocken 3, Small 2, Fish 2+1s, Robinson 2, Purdy 2, Brown 2, Jezz 3(3), Matthews 3(1), Mole 2+1s, Singh 3(3), McCann l+ls, McCall 2(1), Alexiou 2+1s, Smart 1. Opponents: 0G 1.

TODAY'S MATCH: A realistic glance at the table shows that, with the table-toppers almost out of reach, four teams are still in with a chance of making the remaining two Premier Division slots, including today's visitors Swanley, so a close match is in prospect!

WALSINGHAM FLOODLIT CUP FINAL
Buses for the match at Kingsley Stadium next Wednesday will depart from the Lion at 6.30 p.m. sharp. Fares £4. OAP fare £2.50.

ONE, TWO, THREE! COUNTY FOR THE CUP!

Next Saturday: League Div. 2.
County v. Oldhambury
KO 3 p.m.

GOLDEN GOALS: The prize from last week's First Team game against Mannering at the Lane remains unclaimed! Ticket 3010. Will holder please collect, or prize money will be reallocated.

C. Dines (Secretary)

Colts, Reserves or First Team: they've all had their
MURPHY'S CRISPS!
...the real match winners!

7. Warne County Colts v. Swanley

The team that lined up against Swanley for our second home match in the Western Area Qualifiers showed only one change from the team Tommy had printed in the official programme, which went to the printers on Thursday, after training, but there were two positional changes as well.

This was our line-up:

Scott
Brocken Fish Small Robinson
Purdy Brown
Mole Matthews Jezz Singh
Subs: McCann, Alexiou

The big surprise was Scotty in goal, for Tony Bantam. Tony hadn't been dropped. He was travelling with Davie Ledley's Reserve side for an away fixture at Faltham.

'I'm sure we all wish him luck!' Mr Hope said.

Tommy mumbled something about having every confidence that Ally would do as good a job for us as he had against Wolverton, when he kept a clean sheet, but he didn't look pleased.

Then it turned out Ally hadn't brought his boots, because he didn't think he would be playing, and Mr Hope had to get in his car and go and fetch them. Tommy gave Ally a telling-off, but he was half-hearted about it, as though there was some other problem on his mind.

The two positional changes were Cyril swapping with Joe Fish in the middle of the defence, and Moley going out on the wing so that Jezz could go down the middle. As usual, nobody mentioned N. McCann Super Star, who couldn't even get on the park. Tommy said he wanted to stick with an attacking game, and Joe and Harpur were unbalancing the team on the left, because they both liked to go forward and that left no cover. The idea was that Ronnie Purdy would do the ball-winning in front of Joe, and Joe would make runs from behind him, on the right. On the left Harpur would have Cyril to cover him when he went forward, and everybody agreed that it made sense.

Everybody but Alex, that is, and he couldn't say anything because it would have looked bad. He'd been hoping that he would hold his place instead of Joe, having been brought on in the game against Olympic.

Tommy had a word with me before the game. 'You'll get a run second half, son,' he said. 'That's a promise!' which sounded good, except that he added, 'Always providing nothing goes wrong!' which meant it didn't mean very much.

'On the bench, *again*,' Alex said, when we were waiting for the kick-off, kicking our heels on the sidelines.

'Yeah,' I said. 'A pair of Super-subs!'

We started on the attack, and Tommy and Mr Hope seemed to be pleased with the way we went about it. Harpur was spraying the ball about, and with Singhy making tracks down the left and Danny Mole sticking out wide on the right there was a lot more space than we'd had before. Jezz's runs inside coming off his wing had got him goals, but they tangled the front line-up, and prevented Matty from getting space to move.

In the new line-up, the crosses were coming over from both sides, and Matty was getting on the end of them.

With five minutes gone, he did just that, and the ball broke back to Jezz who controlled it neatly, side-stepped his marker, and hit a cracking shot into the side-netting.

Mr Hope and Tommy were both up on their feet cheering.

Then Matty moved on to a through ball

from Ronnie Purdy and slipped it back to Harpur, who was following up from behind. Harpur played the ball behind the back, and Lester Singh only just failed to get on the end of it.

This is how they worked it:

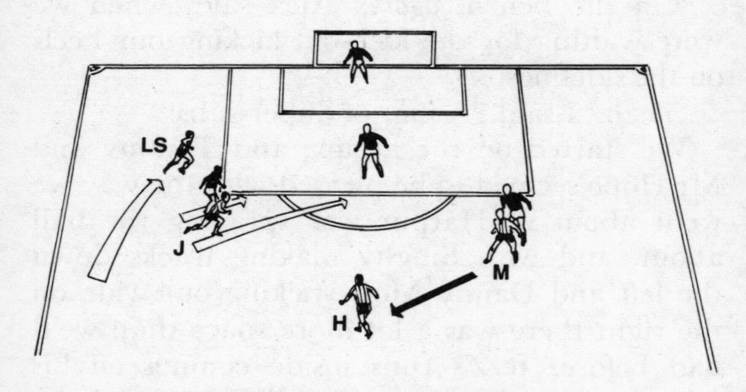

M: Matthews lays the ball back

H: Harper about to play a through ball

J: Jezz's run, taking defender with him

LS: Lester Singh's run

The important thing about this one is the way Jezz's run across the box drew Lester's marker away from him.

Ronnie Purdy took a free kick from the right, and the keeper came out to take the ball off Matty's head. He muffed it, and the ball dropped lose to Danny Mole, who hammered it into the net, which would have been 1–0 to us, but the ref gave a free kick against Matty.

'Good decision,' Tommy said. 'Elbows!'

It cost us a goal, but Matty didn't argue. Then almost exactly the same thing happened, only this time it was Tom Brocken overlapping Danny Mole on the right who put the cross over. The keeper came out quickly, and Matty, trying to get to the ball, crashed into his marker from behind.

Free kick to Swanley, and a talking-to from the ref.

Matty trotted back up the field, with Tommy yelling at him from the dug-out to be careful.

'What's wrong with this team?' Tommy said to Mr Hope. 'Three off in the first game, fighting on the pitch last week, and now another candidate for a red card! Every time we go out, there's trouble with the ref. We'll have to watch it!'

'I don't know,' Mr Hope said wearily. 'Give a dog a bad name, I suppose.'

'Yes . . . the word *has* gone round the refs. We could end up losing out on the Premier Division if we get another ref's report like the one Benny Simms put in.'

They both looked very down in the mouth.

It was difficult, really. Playing with the two wingers putting in crosses from the line, and Harpur and Tom Brocken swinging the ball in high from further back, our game relied on Matty going for the centres. He had the better of their central defender Wictck, but the keeper had spotted it and was coming for everything, in and out of his box, and that meant continual clashes with Matty. It was a high-risk policy, because if Matty got on the end of one, or if the keeper muffed it, then their goal was empty. The other side of that was that the keeper was counting on the ref coming down on his side when they clashed in the air, and so far that was just what had happened.

Tommy talked to Mr Hope, and then he

yelled to Matty to switch with Danny Mole. I think he was afraid Matty might get a yellow card.

The other thing about the high ball that was helping us was that, with the keeper continually coming off his line, the defenders were having to dart back into goal to give him cover, which automatically played us onside.

Matty–Mole worked almost as well as Mole–Matty, though Matty hadn't the same accuracy in his crosses. He got two over. The first the keeper took cleanly, and the next one swirled so that he had to back-pedal and turn the ball over the bar.

Swanley got away two or three times, but both Tom Brocken and Robbo had got on top of their men and Ronnie Purdy was winning a high percentage of what came down the middle.

It was more or less one-way traffic, although they did enough to suggest that they could cause us trouble. The Swanley Coach was up out of the dug-out, yelling at his team, and shortly after they switched their Number 3, Maginn, on to Danny Mole. Maginn made a better job of the aerial battle than Wictck had.

'Getting stuck in a groove,' Tommy said, and he started yelling at Harpur and Ronnie to move the ball about a bit, on the ground.

Then he switched Ronnie and Joe Fish.

It was a good move, because it left us with Cyril and Ronnie killing everything in the middle, and Joe and Harpur coming forward alongside each other, spraying all kinds of different balls at their defence.

'This is it!' Tommy said, banging Mr Hope on the back. 'This is the way we do it! It's coming good!'

I don't think Mr Hope liked being banged. He moved a bit away from Tommy.

Almost immediately a long ball from Joe put Jezz away on the left, with Singhy switching inside. Jezz's neat flick over the back put Singhy clear. The keeper came out and Singhy played the ball inside to Matty coming in from the right, with the keeper stranded.

Matty should have scored, but he blazed the ball over the bar, and we weren't one up when we should have been. Actually we should have been two or three up if we'd got the breaks, but Matty's was the worst miss.

'Somebody stick it in the net!' Tommy yelled. He was getting very excited because we were well on top, but at the same time we hadn't anything to show for it.

Then there was a scramble in their goal, following a long through ball from Joe Fish. The keeper came out and smothered a shot from Jezz and it ran free. Matty and the back went for it and Matty was late in his tackle.

The whistle went, and Matty got the yellow card.

'Oh! Oh! *Oh!*' Mr Hope said miserably.

Tommy was up out of the box, shouting at Matty.

Matty shrugged, and trotted away.

Tommy came over to me. 'Get warmed up,' he said.

G-R-E-A-T!

I was on.

At least, I thought I was getting on. I was running up and down the line and waiting for Tommy to give me the signal, but then Robbo went for a bouncing ball on the left and twisted, somehow. Mr Hope and Tommy went over to him with the bag and they got him on his feet again, but when Tommy came back to the dug-out he told me to put my track suit back on, and he told Alex to warm up, in case Robbo had to come off.

I was back on the bench.

Cyril Small moved across to cover Robbo, who was hobbling about trying to run the injury off, and that meant Joe Fish was pulled back to partner Ronnie Purdy.

They hadn't quite got it sorted out when Swanley made one of their isolated attacks. Their Number 8 played a long ball into the area which Cyril should have got, but he expected Joe to take it out, and Joe didn't.

Just one moment's dozing, and there was the Swanley Number 11, Hamer, clear and going through on goal.

Ally did well. He came out and covered the angle and forced the Number 11 wide and then he managed to get down and block the eventual shot, which was hit at the near post. The ball rebounded off Ally and their Number 7, Ritz, who had got nothing out of Tom Brocken at all, suddenly got on the end of it and volleyed the ball into our net.

0–1 to Swanley.

Tommy was up off the line, yelling at Cyril and Joe. Then Robbo came over signalling that he had to come off. Alex went on for him.

That meant we had used one sub, with only about forty minutes gone, so my chances of getting on didn't look good, whatever Tommy had intended.

Alex went to partner Ronnie and Cyril at the back, and Joe Fish went up to partner Harpur again in midfield, because that was the system that had been working for us before Robbo was hurt.

The goal was Joe's fault. I think he lost concentration with all the switching about. It was his ball and he should have covered it. We were unlucky that they managed to get a goal, because it was a harmless ball that would have been taken out if everybody hadn't been upset by the injury to Robbo.

Mr Hope took Robbo down to the dressing-room to get changed and we sat out the last five minutes of the half with Swanley coming out of their shell now they were a goal in front. The big balls to Danny weren't producing anything, and Matty was tiptoeing round, afraid of getting a red card, and we were going nowhere fast.

The winger who got the goal, Ritz, began to come into it. Tom Brocken was doing his Captain bit, trying to shove everybody forward to get an equalizer before half-time, and little Ritz managed to get some space.

First of all he got away and fired a cross on to the roof of the net, and the next time he nutmegged Cyril, who had come across to take him and fired in a shot which Ally did well to tip round the post for a corner.

Ally took the cross from the corner easily, and then the whistle went.

0–1 at half-time.

I was really down in the dumps when we went to the dressing-room. A win would put Swanley on six points and we knew their last game was against Wolverton, the team that everybody had been beating, so they would finish on nine points. Hume had been one point in front of us going into the fourth series, but they were playing Wolverton, which meant another three points for certain, which would put them on eight with a game to play. It meant that if we didn't get back into the game in the second half we would be stuck on four points at the end of the fourth series, with no chance of making the third Qualifying spot. Our last game, against Queenstown, would be a meaningless competition for who would finish fourth, top of the losers in the group!

'Listen,' Tommy said, when he had us in the dressing-room. 'You are playing well. You're all over them. If you get one goal, you'll get a bagful. This lot isn't going to beat us. They haven't a hope. They are hanging on at the back and they've got nothing to show up front. The way you've played today has been one hundred per cent better than you've played in any game in this competition. All it needs is a goal!'

I don't think he was just saying it. I think he meant it. We were on top, and we should have been two or three goals up at least, against a weak team. Swanley looked worse against us than Wolverton, the team we beat 5–0! Wolverton had shown they could play a bit when they brought on their more skilful players. If they hadn't packed their team with muscles because of our red-card reputation they might have made a much closer game of it. By the time they realized that their little players wouldn't get kicked out of it by a team of hackers, their chance had gone. Swanley had done nothing but score a goal!

'Panic is over!' Tommy said. 'The high ball had them worried, but they've sorted it out. What we need is some along-the-ground stuff, mingled in with the high balls. I want you to take the game and come at them. They finished the half going well, but only because we made a mistake and let them in. They know they are riding their luck. Go out there, play the ball about, run at them, and you'll scare the pants off them!'

Then it was time to go back up the tunnel.

Tommy came over to me, just before the restart.

'Ten minutes, Napper,' he said.

He meant I was getting on . . . so long as nothing happened.

It was the longest ten minutes of my life.

I kept thinking somebody would take a knock and Tommy wouldn't put me on because he would be waiting to see if the player could run it off and then we would get a goal or two and Tommy would decide that he couldn't change the team when the ball was running our way and then I wouldn't get on at all.

Nobody scored. Nobody was hurt.

'You're on,' Tommy said.

'Where?' I said.

'Right down the middle, where you wanted

to be,' Tommy said. 'I'm taking Matty off before he does something and gets a red card. Tell Danny Mole to go back out to the right. The high balls aren't coming off for us, so let's try some of the clever stuff. This team is nothing! We ought to walk through them!'

Striker!

N. McCann Super Star back in business. Well, N. McCann Super-sub anyway. It might be the only chance I would get, so I was determined to take it.

Matty didn't look pleased, coming off, but he gave me a grin. 'Kill 'em!' he said.

The trouble is, that's Matty's game, not mine.

The first five or six balls I got were all Matty/Danny Mole-type efforts, thrown up high into the area. I managed to get on the end of one of them and head it down, but otherwise I wasn't in it.

Tommy was up out of the dug-out, yelling at Harpur and Joe to play the ball on the ground. Then Jezz got the ball, and played the first decent pass I'd had. He came for the return, and I pulled wide of my man and slid it to him and he hit a screamer from the edge of the box.

Their keeper did miracles, clawing it out, and I was just short of picking up the rebound, but the back turned it for a corner.

Harpur went across to take it.

He bent down and placed the ball. Then he stepped back, then he came forward again, picked up the ball, and replaced it. Then he grinned at me, and nodded his head.

B-I-N-G-O!

I trotted towards the penalty spot, jostling Jezz on the way.

'Stay out,' I told him. 'Edge of the area!'

'What?' he said.

'Low ball by the near post,' I said. 'I flick her back, you score. OK?'

He blinked at me.

'It *will* be,' I said. 'I know this routine. Harpur and I have practised it tons of times. Just lie on the edge of the box when everybody dashes in.'

'OK,' he said.

It was one of our old Red Row Stars routines, Secret Sign Number Two. That was why Harpur had made such a dance over repositioning the ball.

Singhy was up, and so were Tom Brocken and Ronnie Purdy and Danny Mole, who had all lined up ready to move in on the cross to the far post.

That was what the Swanley defenders were expecting, because that was what we'd been doing all day.

Instead, Harpur hit the ball low. I was supposed to cut in at the near post and flick it back as their defenders came off the line, but the ball Harpur struck was slightly off target, so I had to lunge back. I managed to nick it with my head. It wasn't an easy ball for Jezz, not more than a half chance, but he is such a good striker it was all he needed. The ball came looping off my head to him, and he volleyed it high into the roof of the net.

G-O-A-L!

Jezz had stayed out, looking as if he would move in late on the cross. The defender who should have been on him had gone back to block the run he was expecting, which never came.

This is how we did it:

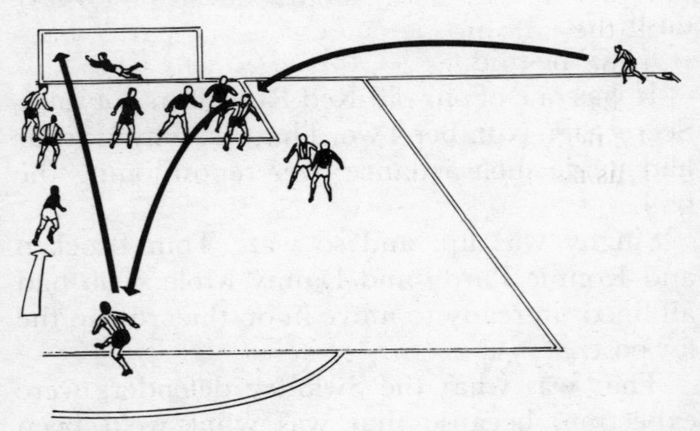

It wouldn't have worked if they hadn't been expecting the high cross for Danny Mole or Tom Brocken. They were expecting it, because nothing else had come over all day, and they were caught napping.

The goal got us going!

Jezz started linking with me and Lester Singh and we were interchanging and switching the ball about on the ground. First Lester got clear and their goalie made a brilliant save. Then Jezz put me through and I beat the keeper to the ball but he pushed me too far wide and I couldn't get it in, so I chipped, and Danny, running in at the far post, headed wide when he had no one to beat. Then Tom overlapped Danny on the right and put in a low-swinging cross. Jezz made a great run and got inside the Number 3, who was moving to cut it out. He took the ball on the chest and lobbed it, all in the one movement, and it went over the goalie and drifted just over the bar, landing on the top of the net, with everybody stranded.

This is what he did:

It was an almost impossible angle to score from, and I was moving for him to play it back, but I could understand why he hadn't. Scoring goals was why he was in the team, so he kept trying to do it. It meant he missed a lot, and sometimes he tried to score himself when he should have passed and ended up looking greedy and foolish, but he still kept pegging away.

'Sorry, Napper,' he said, picking himself up from the ground.

'OK,' I said.

Harpur came into it again. Ronnie played a short ball to him on the edge of the centre circle and Harpur started off on what looked like a run. He pulled to the right, and Lester went streaking away down the wing, drawing the marker with him.

Harpur didn't play it long to Singhy.

Suddenly Alex appeared inside him. Alex had done nothing but sit at the back since he came on, because that was what he had been told to do. But he sensed the opening and timed his run perfectly. The midfield was converging on Harpur and moving right, and Alex came behind Harpur, moving from left to right across the centre circle at a sharp angle.

Harpur back-heeled the ball into his path.

It was done so swiftly that you would think they had been playing together for ages. I don't think Alex even called for the ball. Suddenly there was wide open space down the right, with the defence off balance and Alex haring for the goal, attacking on the side of the field where he wasn't supposed to be.

Alex kept moving right in a diagonal run, forcing Danny Mole's marker to come at him, leaving Danny in a space.

My marker, who was Bridey this time, had to move to cover Danny, but Alex didn't play it to Danny. Instead he switched the ball inside and before Bridey could recover I was on the ball and clear, moving into the area with the keeper coming at me off his line.

This is what happened:

G-O-A-L!

A Napper McCann Brilliant Whamoo Super Goal of the Century at last!

'Neat! Neat! Neat!' Mr Hope yelled.

Tommy was up off the bench cheering and shouting and giving Alex the thumbs up because really it was his run and interchange with Harpur that had made the goal, even if it did go down on the sheet as my goal.

MY GOAL!

2–1 to us!

I'd scored the winner!

Ages and ages and ages I'd been waiting and now I'd come on and done the real Super-sub bit, grabbing the goal that was going to win us the match. We would have seven points going into the last game against Queenstown and we would be odds-on to win it and qualify for the Premier Division.

A goal up, scored by N. McCann Super-sub, and twenty minutes to go.

It was interesting that both subs had played such a big part in the winning goal. Alex had proved what a good player he was by spotting the gap in midfield and making a run which surprised their defenders, and then his through ball had let me in.

Tommy was shouting at us not to go mad and chuck it away. I suppose he was thinking of the Hume game, when we were three up, and let it slip.

Tom Brocken got the message, and he started yelling to Ronnie and Cyril and Joe to keep it tight, and that is what they did. We didn't stop attacking, but nobody went mad. Alex was the one who might have, but he went back into defence and stayed there, with a stupid grin all over his face! Even Harpur settled for the long ball to Lester, and two or three through the middle to me.

2–1 up and hanging on in a game we should have won easily may not sound great, but we knew our Premier Division Qualification might depend on it, and nobody wanted to muck that up. We could all remember the points we'd chucked away against Hume in our first game.

'Good stuff! Good stuff! Good stuff!' Tommy was yelling from the line.

It *was* good stuff. Absolutely the right thing to do, with time running out against a team that really hadn't anything to offer.

The right thing to do, but it changed the pattern of the game, which began to run against us. Well, not *against* us, exactly, because Swanley weren't strong enough to offer any real threat, but they got more possession than they had had at any time during the game. With Harpur and Joe Fish being careful not to come charging out of the back taking risks, Swanley's powder-puff midfielders got a bit of time to dwell on the ball.

It didn't seem to matter, because when they played the ball forward there was a wall across our penalty area, Brocken–Purdy–Small–Alexiou, with Harpur and Joe picking up loose runners from the back when Swanley played it short, and Ally coming off his line and dealing with the long ball as if he had been first-choice keeper all the time.

'Hold them! Hold them!' Tommy was yelling, up out of the dug-out looking at his watch.

Another high ball forward, with their Number 9 chasing a lost cause and Ally coming out confidently to cut it out and Tom Brocken coming across to shield him and . . .

Penalty.

Cyril Small!

It was w-e-i-r-d!

There was no danger at all. Ally was coming to claim it, and Tom was covering in case he fumbled and we had it all sewn up and Cyril just stuck his hands in the air and caught the ball as it went over his head.

Deliberate handball in the area.

Cyril should have been sent off, according to the book, but the ref didn't show him the card. I suppose the ref turned a blind eye because it was obviously so silly, there was nothing on, they hadn't a man anywhere near to it.

'Nobody called,' Cyril mumbled.

Well, he was right, nobody had called, because he had absolutely no chance of getting to the ball if he hadn't jumped up and caught it.

Swanley took the kick.

Ally did really well. He got a hand to the ball, and turned it against the post, but it still ended up in the back of our net.

2–2.

Tommy had his head in his hands, and Cyril was deep in the Cyril-dumps!

We had to go at it all over again, with only five minutes to go and our chance of making the Premier Division slipping away, when we had had it all but sewn up. 'Give it a go!' Tommy shouted.

There was no point in going for a draw. We needed three points, not one.

We kicked off. Everybody charged forward!

Tommy was up out of the dug-out yelling his head off so much that the linesman had a go at him. Even Mr Hope was shouting, 'Give it a go! Give it a go! Give it a go!'

Lester hit their full back on the line, when the keeper was out, and it seemed impossible to miss.

Cyril charged up from the back to try and make good his mistake, and managed to get on the end of a cross from Danny Mole, but he blazed it Cyril-wide, which is wider than anybody else can manage it!

Jezz overdid his tricks twice, when he could have got clear.

I had a header saved at the near post.

Tom Brocken, coming in on a corner, lifted the keeper and gave away a free kick, ruling out Danny's header, which was already on its way to the net.

Then, right at the end, with the ref looking at his watch and the linesmen signalling, the Swanley Number 10 got clear and fired in a blistering shot from the edge of the box. Ally made a brilliant save and turned the ball over the bar.

It was everybody back for the corner, from our point of view, and everybody up from theirs. The ball came across. Ally and Tom went for it together because Ally didn't call. The ball squirmed out of his grasp and down on to the line and Ronnie somehow got a boot to it. The ball ballooned and hit the under-side of the bar and came down. Ally grabbed at it and only succeeded in pushing it against the post. It ran out and their Number 7 got a foot to it and hit it wide, when he should have bust the net.

The whistle went.

2–2.

We'd blown it.

Five points out of four games, instead of seven, and there didn't seem to be any way we could qualify with that.

I was choked. Everybody was, but Tommy was great, praising us like mad, and saying we had played brilliantly, but the luck was against us.

'That first goal!' he said to Harpur. 'Great stuff! You and Napper and Jezz, some combination! Three kids who can think!'

Then he went up to Alex and started praising him for the run that made the second goal for me.

'There'll be no stopping you now, son!' was what he said to me.

He even clapped Cyril on the back and told him not to worry about the goal. It was easy telling Cyril that, but nothing could put it right for him. I have never seen Cyril looking so bad. He was like a zombie-Cyril.

The way Tommy was going on, you would think we had won!

I don't know what he was excited about.

We had played really well, everybody knew

that, but as far as making the Premier Division was concerned, it looked as if we'd blown our chances!

8. Last Chance?

'You should see Napper's Football Career Book, Miss!' our Avril said, grinning. 'He wrote billions and trillions in it this week, and all because he scored a stupid goal at last!'

I don't know why stupid Avril couldn't keep her mouth shut!

'Thank you for reminding me about that, Avril,' Miss Fellows said. 'Well, Napper? I'm sure we'd all like to see what you've written.'

'It's at home, Miss,' I said, looking daggers at Avril.

'Don't forget to bring it in and show me!' Miss Fellows said.

That was a dodgy problem. There wasn't much in my book, not as much as she'd expect there to be, anyway.

I'd written tons about scoring the goal against Swanley, but I had only written about half a page about the game against Olympic. I wasn't even sub for that one, so I didn't think it counted in *my* Football Career, which is what the book was supposed to be about.

My mum always looks at my homework, and she said Miss Fellows wouldn't be satisfied with only half a page and I could do some more, but there wasn't room for any more, because I wrote the Swanley game in after the Olympic game. She said I could take the pages out and rewrite it all, with more about the Olympic match.

'He doesn't want to!' my sister Avril said. 'Old big-head only wants to write about himself!'

That was lucky, because it started Mum on about Avril's school trip essay, and in the argument about that Mum forgot to say I *had* to write some more in my book, she'd just said I *could* and that isn't the same thing!

I didn't want everybody at Red Row to see a stupid Football Career Book that was full of explanations about why I wasn't in the team and scoring goals, but I thought it would be all right if I got picked for the Queenstown game and we won and I was able to write about that.

That is what I was counting on.

Then, on Wednesday, Tommy said we were going to have a team talk, after training, when he would announce the team.

So we all trained, and showered, and dressed, and then we went into the First Team gym, beneath the stand. Everybody was a bit nervous, particularly Cyril. He kept going on about being dropped because he was responsible for the goal that had cost us two points.

'Right!' Tommy said. 'Here's the team for Saturday!'

He paused, and grinned at us.

'Same team that finished the game against Swanley!' he said.

Cyril's face lit up. I thought he was going to do a Cyril-dance, he looked so pleased.

'Robbo is doubtful because of his leg, so he and Matty will be on the bench,' Tommy said.

I didn't look at Matty. It was tough on him, because he had always been on till then, but now it looked as if I was taking his place.

Me! Me in the team! B-R-I-L-L-I-A-N-T.

'I'll tell you *why*, just in case any of you are wondering!' Tommy said. '*Why* is because you got it right, in the second half on Saturday. Everything but the result. There is no way I am going to change things about, when we are beginning to blend. Saturday, you all began to play for each other. Some really good stuff. The high ball had them all over the place in the first half before Robbo had to go off, and the switch to the passing game in the second half was even better. We *won* that game!'

'No we didn't,' Ronnie Purdy muttered. 'We drew, and now we've blown it!'

'Won!' Tommy said. 'If you think we didn't, it is because you don't understand what the game's all about. "Winning" means getting it right. Do that, and the results will come.'

Ronnie bristled.

'I thought it was about who-got-the-most-goals,' he said. 'We didn't. We got two and they got two, and now we can't make it into the Premier Division.'

Tommy grinned. 'Let me read you a surprise result, from last Saturday!' he said. 'Wait for it: HUME COLTS 2 – WOLVERTON 2!'

Nobody could believe it! We all started talking at once. Wolverton had let in ten goals in their first three games, five against us, three against Olympic, and two against Queenstown. They had only scored one. Then they go out for the next game, and score two against the team lying second in the table to get a 2–2 draw, and open the competition up again.

We couldn't understand it.

'It doesn't make sense!' Tom Brocken murmured. 'We beat them hollow.'

'Yeah, well,' Tommy said. 'We should have done the same to Hume, if you remember. They were 3–0 down, and we went to pieces, with half the team sent off. We handed them three goals, with the help of the ref. So Hume aren't that impressive. Wolverton had to make changes, after losing three on the trot, and they must have made the right ones. It is the sort of thing that is *going* to happen in this competition, because Wolverton are like us, a group of players who haven't been together before. Teams like Olympic, who have been winning in the Northern Bell League, are settled. They are going to get results. Wolverton are still sorting things out. They blew it against us, by packing the team with big players, because they thought we were a team of hackers. Remember their game against Olympic? 3–1. We lost by the *same* score. So Wolverton can't be all that bad, can they?'

Tom Brocken had been doing some arithmetic.

'That means Hume have only six points,' he said. 'Right? A win, and three draws.'

'Right,' Tommy said. 'We're next, on five, level with Queenstown. So . . . we can still get second spot or Queenstown can nip in front of us. Beat Queenstown, and you qualify in either second or third spot, depending on the game between Hume and Olympic. It is as simple as that! If you lose, Queenstown qualify along with Hume Colts and Olympic.

'Or Swanley!' Mr Hope said. 'Swanley, not Hume!'

'What?' Tommy said. Nobody had even *thought* of Swanley qualifying, because we all knew they were a nothing team.

'Queenstown would have eight points,' Mr Hope said. 'If Hume *lose* to Olympic, which they probably will, that would leave them on six. Swanley can sneak into third by beating

Wolverton. That would put them on seven points. Olympic would finish first with thirteen points. We would finish second or Queenstown would finish second, one or other of us on eight points, and Swanley would finish third on seven. Hume would only have six, so they would miss out. Of course, if Hume *beat* Olympic they would have nine and then . . . wait a bit, then . . .' Even Mr Hope was getting muddled up, with all the possibilities.

'In other words, it is too close to call!' Tommy said, looking a bit puzzled. It is the kind of thing Mr Hope loves, because he is a Headmaster and he can do maths, which most footballers can't.

'It's simple enough,' Tom Brocken said. 'If we beat Queenstown, we qualify. If we lose to Queenstown we have only five points and we are out!'

'We'll pulverize them!' Cyril shouted, only half-way through the shout it changed into a squeak. 'Well, I think we will anyway,' he added, because he knew who was going to be blamed for playing netball if we didn't qualify!

We had to beat Queenstown to qualify for the Premier Division.

It was our last chance.

OWEN LANE STADIUM

WARNE COUNTY COLTS

v.

QUEENSTOWN

Brontley League: Western Area Qualifying Competition

KO 11.15 a.m.

PRODUCTION OF THIS PROGRAMME SPONSORED BY

THE BRONTLEY BUILDING SOCIETY

NOTES FROM OUR CHAIRMAN, Mr Duncan Murphy

I would like to take this opportunity to say something about the sponsors of this competition, the Brontley Building Society, and, in particular, my old friend Jack Dade, Chairman of Queenstown, who are our visitors today. Jack is the man behind our sponsor's involvement, and I am sure he will get a thrill seeing the youngsters on the park today and the mums and dads and grans and grandads who have turned up to support them. Thank you, Brontley Building Society. Thank you, Jack Dade!

Duncan Murphy

TOMMY SAYS ...

We are on our way! Although the result of last week's game against Swanley was disappointing, the performance was not! Our very young team is coming together well, with incisive play from Mole and Singh down the flanks and a solid defence built round Skipper Brocken, Small and Purdy. Brown and Fish are linking intelligently to complement the thrust of our young goal 'star', Jezz, surely one of the 'finds' of the season. A feature of the Swanley game was our ability to change our game in the second half, when Swanley had managed to counter our first-half route-one attacks. McCann, coming on as sub, provided us with a new set of options and scored an excellent goal. The other big 'plus' for me as a Manager took place elsewhere, at Faltham, where young Tony Bantam stepped into the breach caused by the injury to keeper Norrie Swinburne in the Reserves. Tony conceded five goals, but did enough to justify his inclusion, quite an achievement for a boy of his age. Although still very much a stripling, what Tony lacks in size he makes up for in sheer ability ... just watch this boy (grow) go!

Watch the Colts, for the stars of tomorrow!

TOMMY

WALSINGHAM FLOODLIT CUP FINAL REPLAY
Tickets for the replay against Alyson Town are on sale after this morning's match from the kiosk behind the reserved enclosure. The match will be played to a finish, with extra time and penalties if required.

Coaches will be available, details to be announced

C.Dines (Secretary)

COUNTY v. DORSINGHAM TOWN
A coach will leave the ground at l.30 p.m. for our League game this afternoon. Some places are still available.

Fares £2. OAP, unemployed and schoolboy £1.75

County scarves and souvenirs are available as usual from the kiosk.

TODAY'S TEAMS

WARNE COUNTY COLTS (Black & white stripes, black shorts)	**v.**	**Queenstown** (Blue shirts, blue shorts)
Scott 1	1	Brant 1
Brocken 2	2	Cooler 14
Alexiou 3	3	Jacks 3
Small 4	4	Wilton 4
Fish 5	5	Miller 6
Purdy 6	6	Aspin 5
Brown 7	7	Dunphy 7
Mole 8	8	Allop 8
McCann 9	9	Streeter 9
Jezz 10	10	Cousins 10
Singh 11	11	Formley 11
Robinson 12	12	Taylor 2
Matthews 14	13	Jonson 12

Match Officials
Ref: B. Simms. Linesmen: K. Yantley, B. Ogg

BRONTLEY LEAGUE

WESTERN AREA QUALIFYING COMPETITION

Fourth Series Results

Warne Colts	2	Swanley	2
Hume Colts	2	Wolverton	2
Queenstown	3	Olympic YC	3

Fifth Series Fixtures

Warne Colts	v.	Queenstown
Wolverton	v.	Swanley
Hume Colts	v.	Olympic YC

League Table	P	W	D	L	F	A	Pts	
Olympic YC	4	3	1	0	13	7	10	+6
Hume Colts	4	1	3	0	7	6	6	+1
Warne Colts	4	1	2	1	11	8	5	+3
Queenstown	4	1	2	1	6	5	5	+1
Swanley	4	1	1	2	5	7	4	-2
Wolverton	4	0	1	3	3	12	1	-9

WARNE COUNTY COLTS APPEARANCES AND GOAL-SCORERS

Bantam 2, Scott 2, Brocken 4, Small 3, Fish 3+1s, Robinson 3, Purdy 3, Brown 3, Jezz 4(4), Matthews 4(1), Mole 3+1s, Singh 4(3), McCann 1+2s(1), McCall 2(1), Alexiou 2+2s, Smart 1. Opponents: OG 1

TODAY'S MATCH:

As will be seen from the above table, visitors Queenstown have everything to play for today, as have the Colts. Any two out of four teams could qualify for the new Premier Division, in addition to Olympic YC, whose place is already secure. The outcome will depend on the fifth and final games in this section. Goal difference may well decide the crucial placings, so let's hope the Colts' top strikers, Singh and Jezz, are on song!

9. Warne County Colts v. Queenstown

This was our line-up for the game against Queenstown:

Scott
Brocken Purdy Small Alexiou
Fish Brown
Mole McCann Jezz Singh
Subs: Matthews, Robinson

The saddest sight of all was Tony Bantam, sitting in the grandstand. Mr Hope was very upset about Tony. He said that Davie Ledley should never have played such a young kid in the Reserves, even if it was a last-minute emergency when their keeper reported unfit on the morning of the match. Tony had done his best, but he let in five, and his ribs were so badly bruised into the bargain that he couldn't play for us against Queenstown, which was *important*. The rotten Reserve game had only been a friendly! Tommy had arrived at the ground to find his star goalie already gone with the Reserves, and a note from Davie Ledley telling Tommy what he had done.

'*That's* why Tommy Cowans looked so grim before last week's game!' Cyril said.

I think Mr Hope realized he had told us things he wasn't supposed to. He told us not to mention it to anyone, because relations were a bit strained at the club, particularly with Tony being hurt. We didn't know what he meant by relations. Maybe Tony Bantam's dad was cross about it, or something, like Wally Usiskin's.

'My dad would do a dance if I got in the Reserves!' Cyril said.

'You're lucky to be in *this* team, after deciding to play netball in the penalty area last week, Cyril!' Mr Hope said, and that shut Cyril up.

It was tough on Tony, but we thought Ally wouldn't let anybody down.

'No sense in changing things round when they are going well!' Tommy said in the dressing-room.

He told us to keep things simple.

'Play it to a shirt,' he said. Then he told Ronnie and Cyril that their job was to button up the back. Joe and Harpur were to use every chance they got to come forward. Jezz and I were to switch about in the middle like last week, so our markers would keep losing us. Singhy and Danny were to go wide, but when one of them had the ball the other was to be ready to come in for the cross to the far post. 'Up to now, we've been playing with at least one big striker,' Tommy said. 'We could count on knock-downs. That won't happen this week. I'm taking a gamble on Napper and Jezz instead, because they did so well together last week. They are better suited to the ball on the ground. It is up to them to do something with it, if the rest of you can lay on the supply. The beauty of it is that we have Matty on the bench. If the new system doesn't work, we pull one of the small strikers off, and go back to the high-ball routine.'

Tommy didn't say so, but I knew that pulling somebody off meant *me*, not Jezz. Anyway, it wasn't going to happen, because we were going to combine together and be brilliant! We'd proved the team played better that way last week, so there was no reason why we couldn't do it . . . except the other team!

We didn't know anything about Queenstown except that, like us, they were a new team. They had lost to Swanley in their first match, then drawn with Hume, then beaten Wolverton and drawn with Olympic. So they were getting better all the time, sorting things out.

'They are the only team to take a point from Olympic!' Harpur said when we were talking about the game in the dressing-room. 'Forget the Swanley result.'

'Maybe Olympic are slipping!' I said.

It was funny. We had all thought Olympic would be the worst team, because they were just a boy's club from the Northern Bell League, and not attached to one of the top sides. In fact they were a settled team, used to playing together, and they had been up against teams who were still being sorted out by their managers, with new players coming in every week.

'It will be different next season, when the League gets going!' Harpur said.

'It is this season I'm worried about!' Cyril said, getting the Cyril-fidgets again!

It was cold and clear when Tom Brocken led us out. We got a cheer from all our fans and then we trotted down to the goal at the clock end. Scotty went in goal and Alex and I hit crosses for him, whilst the others passed about amongst themselves.

Then Queenstown came out.

They had blue shirts with a 'Q' on the breast, for Queenstown, and they looked pretty much like us, three or four big players and the rest just ordinary. We hadn't been able to watch them, but Tommy had been told they were a footballing side, not hackers or long-ball bombers, and could play a bit.

The ref came out.

'H-e-l-p!' Ronnie Purdy said.

We hadn't realized who the ref was. It was

Mr Simms, who had sent three players off when we played Hume, and cost us the game with his decisions.

'Never mind the ref!' Tommy bawled from the touch-line. I think Mr Simms heard Tommy, because he grinned all over his face.

I think Tommy was worried in case everybody got ref-itis, and started listening for the whistle instead of getting on with the game. That can happen, when a ref makes a few bad decisions, or loses control of a game early on, or simply makes too much of a fuss about imposing himself on the game, giving niggly free kicks instead of letting the play flow.

We needn't have worried.

The game went off at a hundred miles an hour. First Danny Mole broke away on the right and hit a screamer at their keeper, who clawed it out of the air, making a great save. Then Moley did it again, but this time he flighted over a cross for Singhy, who came in at the far post and headed narrowly wide. It was exactly what Tommy had told them to do, missing out the middle and crossing to each other.

Queenstown didn't sit back and take it. They were as eager to win as we were. Their Number 7, Dunphy, got away on the right, dummied inside Alex and put in a cross that beat Ally as he came off his line and Cyril had to head it behind for a corner, as their Number 11 steamed in to finish it off, with Tom Brocken nowhere.

Tommy was up in the dug-out, yelling at Tom Brocken, but he didn't come on to the touch-line. He must have remembered who the ref was!

The corner didn't come to anything and from Ally's throw-out Singhy got away on the wing. We were used to Singhy sprinting clear, but this time their Number 3, Jacks, was able to match him stride for stride, and eventually Singhy ran the ball behind for a goal-kick.

Tommy was up and yelling at him to switch the ball into the box, where Danny had turned up at the far post, as ordered. Singhy waved his arm in acknowledgement. Jacks was grinning all over his face.

Singhy got two more runs, his usual style, head down, and each time Jacks closed him down and forced him wide, the first time turning the ball into touch for a throw that came to nothing, and next time, when Singhy tried to turn inside, dispossessing him and making a run of his own. It was the first time Singhy had come up against a back who could take him for speed, and he didn't like it.

Singhy stood there, hands on hips, shaking his head in disbelief, with Jacks steaming away from him upfield.

Jacks went straight at the heart of the defence, drawing Harpur into the tackle and playing a swift ball inside to their Number 10, then taking the return and playing it wide as Alex came across to cut him out. The ball was switched across field to their Number 11, Formley, and he fired in a cross that Ronnie Purdy managed to turn over for another corner with their Number 9, a big red-headed lad called Streeter, breathing down his neck.

Jacks ran over to take the corner.

He surprised everyone by firing it in low, and Streeter cut across Alex, who'd moved off the line to intercept. Streeter only got a touch on the ball but it was enough to send it smacking against the near post and out for a goal-kick. We were lucky really, because they worked the corner so neatly that we could have gone a goal down.

'Like your Plan Number Two, Napper,' Jezz said to me. 'Only the direct version.'

Harpur and Cyril and I had been through the old Red Row plans with Jezz, and we had worked a bit on them in training, though Tommy didn't go for it. Tommy said there would be time enough to work on set pieces when we'd learnt the basics, and the drawing-book stuff could wait. He didn't say so, but I think he was worried by the way Davie Ledley had tried to drill things into us early on, which had confused us. It is one thing having plans when you play together every day at school, as we did at Red Row, and another when you only get together on training nights.

'*Concentrate on your natural game.*'

'*Play it to a shirt.*'

'*Read the game.*'

That was the kind of thing Tommy kept saying. It didn't seem like coaching at all, certainly not the way Mr Hope used to do it at Red Row, but it was probably good because the team was combining better every time as we got used to each other, and we might not have been able to do it if he had given us packs of instructions.

Jezz was the exception to the rule. All we ever heard Tommy say to him was '*Be selfish*', which was different from what he was telling the rest of us.

The thing was, when Jezz got the ball to his feet, he was brilliant!

When he got it.

Jezz and I were both a bit anxious, because when we came forward it was still high-ball stuff, missing us out, aimed at the far post for either winger coming in. We were in the team to work the ball through the middle, but the rest of the team seemed to have forgotten about feeding us balls we could work with.

Jezz turned that around!

He started showing Queenstown what he could do. First he took a flick on from me, after Ronnie Purdy had belted the ball anywhere out of defence. Danny Mole had come off his man and was screaming for the ball but Jezz turned his man and, seeing the goalie coming off his line, chipped him from miles out. The ball beat the goalie all ends up, hit the bar, came down on the line and the goalie, scampering back, almost turned it into the net, grabbing it at the second attempt when we were all ready to yell, 'Goal!'

Jezz put his head in his hands. He couldn't believe that the ball hadn't gone in.

'Good ball, Napper!' Tommy called out from the dug-out. I thought it wasn't anything special, but I was pleased because he'd told me that that was what he wanted me to do, feed Jezz the simple ball, and I thought nobody would have noticed it.

Next time Joe fed the ball to his feet Jezz did a kind of shuffle on the ball and flicked it round his back and he was away.

Outside the back, inside the Number 6 coming across, feinted to go inside, then outside again, heading for the corner flag as though he'd lost control and then, just when it seemed he had overrun the ball, he back-heeled it to Danny Mole, who was steaming in from the wing. Danny hit the ball like a rocket.

This is how Jezz worked it with Danny:

It looked a goal all the way, but their keeper flung himself sideways and tipped the ball round the post.

Tommy was up off his seat, clapping.

Jezz was brilliant, the trouble was he was doing all the things I wanted to do, and he was doing it so well that I couldn't get a look-in. It wouldn't have been so bad, but half of Red Row School was in the stand, because they'd all heard I was in the team and it was our make or break match.

The game was well balanced, nobody was giving anything away. Danny Mole was looking lively down the right, where it seemed as if he'd found his best position, after doing not-very-much in the centre when he was paired with Matty. The others had remembered that Jezz and I were on the pitch, and they started giving us the ball, which meant we could go at the defence. The weak spot going forward was what was usually our strength – Singhy. Jacks had him bottled up on the left, and he started trying to come inside to leave room for Harpur to overlap. The idea was that Jacks would follow Singhy inside and that would leave room for Harpur to overlap, or even Alex if he got the chance.

Jacks didn't fall for it.

He stayed put, and then when Queenstown got the ball he was able to move forward unchallenged, turning the tables on Harpur and Alex, who were supposed to be attacking *his* space.

Harpur didn't like it. There was no use gunning for Singhy, who can't tackle for butternuts, so he shouted at me to cover when Jacks made his runs.

We wound up with Singhy wandering inside, and me pulling wide on our left to defend against *his* back, which wasn't the way we wanted to play at all. It cut off the one-twos with Jezz which were the reason for my being in the team! Singhy doesn't know the meaning of a one-two, he just puts his head down and sprints.

I was being pulled further and further back, wide on the left-hand side, and even then I wasn't coping. If Jacks was fast enough to out-sprint Singhy, there was no way I could stop him, short of bringing him down, which I couldn't risk with a ref like Mr Simms, who liked using red cards.

Jacks was all over the place. He got away from Harpur after he had bypassed me, fired in a cross that big Streeter connected with again, although he couldn't turn it into a goal. Then he nutmegged me and made a break on his own, pulling Harpur off his man again, and turning the ball inside. Ally was awake, and came out to smother the ball at Streeter's feet, but it was a near thing.

Ronnie Purdy could see where the trouble was coming from, and he began coming off Streeter to back Harpur, but that was dangerous because Streeter was fast and, with the extra space he had, he soon had us in more trouble.

He got clear twice. The first time he mishit his shot and Scotty collected easily, and the next time he smacked it over the bar, when really he should have scored.

Queenstown were on top, and the game was slipping away from us.

Tommy and Mr Hope saw what was happening, and Tommy made a brave decision. I thought if he brought anyone on it would be Robbo, to stiffen up the defence, but Tommy didn't do that. The trouble in the defence was happening because of the problem up front, where we were losing out on the left side. Next thing we knew Singhy was walking off, and Matty was running on, yelling instructions from Tommy, with a grin all over his face.

Singhy off, not *me*, so Tommy must still believe Jezz and I could do it.

Then I realized that with Matty on he would be in the centre and guess who was going to be shuffled to a full-time marking job on a back I couldn't keep pace with? Tommy should have brought Robbo on, not Matty, then I would have been all right. Second half, he would bring Robbo on, and I would be O-U-T!

That isn't what happened.

Matty went wide on our right, and Danny Mole came over to the left, and I got orders to get back up there with Jezz and do something! It was great! Great . . . but *risky*. Danny hadn't done much when we played him as an emergency defender in the first game, but then he was tucked in at the back and his positional sense let him down. This time Tommy had told him to do a man-to-man job, stopping Jack's runs before the back could get into his stride, and going forward wide himself when he got the chance. It meant that the balance of our team would still be an attacking one. Bringing on Robbo in place of Singhy would have changed that and kept us on the defensive.

It must have been a big decision for Tommy, but that is what he did!

Instead of brushing my tackles aside, Jacks found himself getting the ball and Danny Mole at the same time, and he didn't fancy it. After the third time, he started yelling at the ref but Mr Simms took no notice. Danny was coming in hard every time, but they were good tackles.

Tommy signalled Harpur to move up, which was good because he'd been pushed right back, expecting Jacks to come at him in the clear, and moving up gave him more chance to spring something when we got possession.

Twice he did it.

The first time he put Danny clear of Jacks, and Danny centred, but the goalie took it off Jezz's head as if he could catch stuff like that all day. Danny should have played the ball in low.

The next time Harpur brought the ball forward himself and then released me. I drew my man on and then played a near ball through to Jezz, who put his head down and went for goal, ignoring the reverse pass which would have put me clear. Their Number 6, who'd come off me, put in a hard tackle. Jezz did a thriller-diller dive and got up yelling for a penalty. He was the only one who yelled.

'Sorry, Napper!' Jezz said. I was mad. I'd set it up and I could have been on the end of it with my second goal for County in our most important game, and it had all gone to waste.

Tommy yelled at him too.

The next time Jezz got the ball he looked for me, and played a good pass inside and for once I had a chance. It wasn't much of a one, but I got some force in the shot, and the keeper did well to grab it at the second attempt.

'That's it!' Jezz said, and Harpur clapped him for making the pass, when he could have gone on himself.

The keeper played a long ball down the centre to Streeter, who back-headed it over Ronnie Purdy straight into Formley's path.

BANG!

Goal.

1–0 to Queenstown.

It was a simple goal out of nothing, nobody's fault, but it looked as if it had turned the game.

Suddenly they were all over us, rushing in from all angles. They had two or three near misses and both their flankers started to play. Ronnie and Cyril were having it tough, and the tackles started flying in. Alex got himself booked for a wild tackle on Formley and then Ronnie, coming in late on a run by the Number 10, Cousins, took man and ball at the same time, two-footed.

He got a real telling-off from Mr Simms, arms waggling all over the place, and a yellow card from our favourite off-you-go referee.

Scotty had his wall positioned, and the ball was twenty metres out. We thought we had everything covered but Cousins, who'd done almost nothing up to then but earn the free kick, hit a swerver. Ally got his fingers to it but he couldn't stop it. The ball hit the under-side of the bar and ended up bouncing down behind the line before anyone could get back to hook it out. Ally wasn't really to blame, but I thought Tony Bantam might have got it, if he hadn't been resting his bruised ribs in the stand because of Davie Ledley.

2–0 to Queenstown.

Tommy was up on the touch-line yelling at us.

It didn't do any good because everything had gone to pieces. It was real backs-to-the-wall stuff, with Tom Brocken out-tricked on one side of the field by Formley and Ronnie scared stiff of a red card on the other. Cousins was all over the place suddenly, coming alive because of his goal, and Ronnie was missing his tackles. The only plus mark we had was Cyril, who was picking up everything that came his way, and finally getting a grip on big Streeter, after the damage was done.

Half-time.

2–0 down.

I thought for sure that Tommy would bring Robbo on, stick Matty down the middle, and go back to the way we used to play, which meant I'd be off.

Tommy brought Robbo on, but he didn't sub me!

It was Alex who came off, and Tommy switched Tom Brocken and Robbo so that Robbo could take Formley, who had been beating Tom. He told Tom to take Dunphy out, the way Danny Mole had been dealing with Jacks, so that they'd have nothing at all wide on their right, where most of the danger had come from.

'Forget Jacks,' he told Harpur. 'Take Cousins out, the Number 10. Ten minutes should do it. He is an in-and-out player, but he's going well now because he got the goal. Keep him out of it till he loses interest again, then up you go and do your real job, feeding Napper and Jezz.'

Then he told Jezz to keep looking for me. 'Once in a while, lay it back for somebody else, son,' he added.

'You told me to be selfish,' Jezz said.

'When that works, it works, son,' he said. 'But they've spotted it, haven't they? They know you are the one we're expecting to score. What they don't know is that Napper is in the business as well. They don't know, because nine times out of ten he's been putting you in, and there's only been an odd ball the other way. Doesn't matter which of you scores, son, so long as we get one quickly, and get back in the game.'

Then Mr Hope came in the dressing-room and said something to Tommy. Tommy groaned and turned to us. 'Hume are one up against Olympic,' he said.

There was a dead silence.

How could they be? Olympic hadn't lost a game in the competition . . . but then neither had Hume, and Hume were like us, a team that was still finding its feet. If Hume won, they would have nine points and be sure of qualifying.

'No matter!' Tommy said. 'Hume and Olympic are likely to qualify anyway. You *can* do it if you beat this lot. Right? There are three qualifying places, and right now we are playing Queenstown for the last one!'

Nobody said anything. We were 2–0 down. There wasn't much we could say.

We went out for the second half, knowing we needed three goals to win it, and nothing going in at the other end.

On the way up the tunnel, Tommy tugged my sleeve.

'Napper!' he said. 'Time you did your own

stuff son, instead of standing there admiring Jezz. You can't pass the responsibility on to him all the time, you know!'

Then he added: 'Be selfish!'

I went out thinking, Maybe he's right. Maybe strikers have to be like that, some of the time. Maybe I had been sitting back and praising myself for playing for the team, while Jezz was taking all the risks and getting all the glory. Jezz looked bad when he missed in situations where he could have laid the ball on for someone else, but everybody cheered when he scored.

I had forty-five minutes to do it in.

All I needed was a hat trick!

10. Hat Tricks?

Five minutes gone in the second half.

Joe Fish moved out of defence, and switched the ball left to Harpur, just before he was clobbered by their Number 3, who had come upfield and was anxious to stop Joe getting the ball wide to Matty, whom he should have been marking.

It should have been a free, but the ref took a quick look and then he let play go on, because we were in possession and moving forward, and their defence was exposed.

Harpur took it on the edge of the centre circle, just inside our half. He looked up, and saw that Matty was clear.

A deep, deep ball wide to the right.

Matty ran on to it and hit a low-angled ball hard across the face of the box so the keeper couldn't claim it.

I was steaming in to meet the ball, clear of my man.

Thump!

G-O-A-L!

G-O-A-L! G-O-A-L! G-O-A-L!

The Napper McCann Super Header of the Century. I met it full stretch, at about the penalty spot, and the ball rocketed into the back of the net.

I know it did, because I've seen it.

Miss Fellows had brought her video camera to the match, and she was filming from the stand. She showed us her Big Match film in school on Monday.

This is what my rocket header goal looked like on the TV in the hall. We had all the Senior classes in to see it, and everybody cheered!

Mr Hope talked all the Senior classes through the goal and made Miss Fellows run the film back so we could see how the ref's decision to let play flow led to the goal, when otherwise it would have been a nothing-much-on free kick in our own half.

We decided Mr Simms was maybe not such a bad referee after all!

One to us!

Everybody mobbed me!

'Two more like that, Napper!' Tom Brocken said, when we were lining up.

That's what I thought too. Get two more, which would be my hat trick, and we would win the game and I would have got us into the Premier Division all by myself in the only game where they'd let me play in my proper position, Star Striker.

It is what would have happened in one of Cyril's soccer comics, where people are always getting hat tricks to win the cup final despite the goalie being blackmailed.

Instead, I got three chances one after the other, and missed the lot.

First Harpur did his stuff again and put me clean through, but the goalie came off his line and narrowed the angle and I hit the side-netting.

Then I took their Number 5 on and beat him on the edge of the area and wham-bammed a rocket in, but the ball hit the angle of the post and the crossbar and came back to Jezz, who got his feet mixed up and missed it. He couldn't believe that he had. It was the easiest chance we had had in the competition.

'It's going to come! It's going to come!' Tom Brocken was yelling from the back. He had a run himself, turned the ball in to Jezz and Jezz fooled them all into thinking he was going himself and then played it in to me, coming in at the far post, and I got on the end of the ball with another flying header.

I don't know how the keeper got it. He went down, to his left and clawed the ball up in the air from almost ground level, and it looped over the bar.

'Again, Napper! Again!' Tom yelled, clapping his hands.

The corner was cleared and the ball went down the other end of the field. Ronnie fastened on to it with Streeter rushing in on him and Ronnie turned and played the ball back to Ally.

Too softly!

Streeter belted past Ronnie and got to the ball just before Ally, steering it round him, and then he finished off tapping it into the empty net!

Goal!

3–1 to Queenstown.

Ally picked the ball out of the net, looking disgusted. He didn't look where he was booting it, and the ball hit Mr Simms on the back of the neck and flattened him.

Ally stood there gaping at what he had done.

3–1 down, and he had flattened the famous sending-off ref!

Mr Simms got up, rubbing the back of his neck. He put his teeth back in . . . the unexpected blow had knocked them out . . . and then he blew his whistle and pointed to the centre spot, for the restart.

No sending-off!

We thought Ally was lucky, but maybe it was to do with the way the game was going. There had been lots of niggle in the Hume match, and when Robbo knocked the little Number 8 over after their goal it looked like part of the niggle, which is why he got his marching orders. Mr Simms was almost at the half-way when Ally's punt hit him, so he must have realized that it couldn't have been deliberate.

'Go at them! Go at them!' Tommy was yelling from the dug-out, and there really wasn't anything else we could do, 3–1 down with twenty-five minutes to go, and almost no chance of getting the three goals we needed to win.

That is what we all thought.

Everybody swarmed forward, leaving Cyril and the goalie at the back.

Robbo had a shot charged down in the area when it looked a cert goal.

Tom Brocken, coming in at the far post, headed over the bar when Matty, who was a few yards outside him, would have had an easy tap in.

I put Jezz through and he beat the goalie, but fired wide.

Then Streeter got away on the left and Cyril had two of them coming at him, because Cousins was free in the middle. Streeter drew Cyril and flighted the ball across and Cousins got up and met it, but Ally took the ball in a full-length dive.

If it had gone in we would have been finished.

Their Manager was up on the line, shouting something to his players.

'What's that about?' I asked Matty, who was nearest to him.

'Olympic,' he said. '3–1 up against Hume!'

Hume had been 1–0 in front at half-time, surprising everybody, but Olympic must have pulled it back. If they could, we could, except that Queenstown were finishing the competition looking a lot stronger than Hume ever had. The only match Queenstown had lost had been their opening one against Swanley, who, we reckoned, were one of the weakest sides in it.

The Hume v. Olympic score didn't seem to matter that much to me, but the Queenstown players were all shouting it to each other, and it made a difference to them.

They pulled back. Even Streeter stopped wandering about trying to draw Cyril, and dropped back to pick up Harpur, freeing the player who *had* been doing it to tuck in in defence.

Fifteen minutes to go. 3–1 down. Losing.

Then . . .

Harpur to Ronnie, who had come storming through. Ronnie to Jezz. Jezz did a bit on the ball, fiddled with it, looked like he'd lost it, and then chipped it in from the edge of the area.

I met it on the volley, just outside the box.

WHAM!

WHAM-BAM! ZAMEROO!

G-O-A-L!

Goal all the way from the lethal boot of N. McCann Super-sub turned Super Striker, on his way to the hat trick that would save the game and get us into the Premier Division . . . well, it would if we got *two* goals, my hat trick plus one. We knew we had to win the game, not draw it . . .

3–2 to them, ten minutes to go.

They were hanging on by a bootlace.

We thought they would come and have a go at us, because they needed a win as much as we did, but they didn't. Jacks was lying at the back, marshalling things, and Streeter and Dunphy and Formley, their dangermen, were playing square across the park.

They took Cousins off and put a guy like an elephant on. They stuck him right in the middle of the defence to cut off the balls we'd been floating to Matty coming in at the far post.

Jezz took a crack from right outside the area, and the goalie sprawled to his right, and sent it for a corner.

Plan Number Two again.

Jezz on the edge of the area, me making a run in front of Jacks, who was on the post, with the idea of flicking it back.

Jezz was dancing about, ready to make a name for himself.

I started my run as Harpur hit the ball.

Boom!

One minute I was running, and the next the Elephant had flattened me, right in the box.

Penalty!

But it wasn't.

I suppose Mr Simms missed it in the bodies, but I was expecting the linesman's flag to go up. No flag. Jacks met Harpur's low cross, and volleyed it high on to the touch-line terrace, time-wasting.

Five minutes to go. Still 3–2 to Queenstown.

Cyril, who had come forward now as well, picked up a loose clearance on the centre spot. He saw me moving wide of him, and played a square ball.

They were all funnelling back.

There was nothing on, so I put down my head and ran.

The Elephant lumbered out to clatter me, and I feinted left and shoved the ball right. Then Jacks was closing in, and I turned him. I was in the box and closing in on the keeper, going to get my Super Star hat trick. The keeper came out and I shot and the ball hit him in the chest and broke loose to the man who was following up . . .

. . . Cyril!

If there is one player you *wouldn't* want it to be, in that situation, needing two goals in five minutes, it is Cyril I-Am-Going-To-Play-For-Man.-United Small.

But it *was* Cyril, reading the play and matching my run after he laid the ball off.

I thought old Cyril would blaze it over the bar in true Cyril style, but he played it firmly along the ground.

G-O-A-L!

Goal! Goal! Goal! A Cyril Small Super Striker goal! I don't think anyone was more amazed than Cyril to see it nestling in the back of the net. Mr Hope said it was a neat finish, when we saw it on Miss Fellow's video, but Dribbler said Cyril should get a freeze-frame of it and stick it on his bedroom wall, in case he never got another one.

3–3.

And we needed a win.

Two minutes to go.

Jezz got clear, waltzed round the keeper, and banged the ball into the side-netting. He was down on his knees pounding the ground, but that didn't help anyone.

Then Matty headed over.

Then C. Small Super Striker turned up again and banged the ball about twenty metres over the bar, when anybody else would have scored.

N. McCann headed straight into the keeper's hands from a metre out.

Harpur went down under an Elephant rush in the area, but we didn't get the penalty and really we were lucky nobody was sent off, because we were all shouting at the ref.

Then the whistle went.

3–3!

The Queenstown players and their Manager were out dancing on the pitch.

'What's wrong with them?' Harpur said. We couldn't understand it. We both needed a win to qualify, and all we'd got was a draw. We were on six points and so were they.

The Elephant came up to me and stuck his hand out. 'Good game, Striker!' he said. 'See you in the Premier Division next season!'

'Eh?' I said.

'You bet!' he said. Then he grinned at me. 'Wolverton 3 – Swanley 3,' he said. 'It's a final result! They kicked off before us.'

It took a moment to sink in.

Hume losing . . . that left them on six. Swanley drawing . . . that left them on five.

'Six points?' I said.

'Six points and we both qualify!' he said.

'But . . . but . . .'

'Goal difference!' he said. 'Hume lost, so they stay on six points and their goal difference goes *down*. They were plus one like us, now they'll be minus something, right?'

'Y-e-s!' I said, beginning to bubble. 'They were 3–1 down so they'll be . . .'

'Minus one goal difference,' the Elephant said. 'We are on six points, with plus one goal difference. You've got six points, with plus three! That means Olympic comes first, you are second, and we wind up third! We all qualify. Brilliant, isn't it?'

We had qualified in second spot with plus three goals making all the difference!

Everybody seemed to wake up to it at once! Suddenly our team were dancing and shouting too.

Then Harpur said: '*If* Hume lost,' meaning, what-happens-if-Hume-stormed-back-in-the-last-five-minutes-and-won?

'They were 3–1 down with only a few minutes left!' the Elephant said.

'So were we!' Harpur said.

That stopped us for a minute. Hume would have seven points and . . .

'We qualify anyway!' Cyril shouted. 'We'd be third, instead of second, but we've still made it because of the plus 3. Queenstown *could* be out, but we *are* in!'

He started doing a Cyril-dance and Robbo and Tony Bantam, who'd run out on to the field, joined in!

The Elephant's jaw dropped. He turned round to tell his mates they could be out of it after all, and then there was a big cheer from the crowd round the tunnel and somebody shouted.

'They *lost*! They *lost*! Hume lost!'

Queenstown started celebrating all over again! Everybody was running round clapping everybody on the back, because both teams had qualified for the Premier after all.

Then it was down to the dressing-room to change and out to go home and all the Red Row kids were there and I was telling everybody about how I'd thought I would get a hat trick and my three goals would mean we'd win and I hadn't but we had won anyway.

'Hat trick?' Cyril said, bouncing up to me. 'What *is* a hat trick?'

'Three goals!' I said. 'Anybody knows that.'

'Right!' Cyril said. 'How many goals did you score altogether in the competition?'

'Three,' I said. 'One against Swanley last week, and two today. 'But that is three goals . . . not a hat trick. A hat trick is three in one game!'

'We got into the Premier Division on goal

difference,' Cyril said. 'What was our goal difference?'

'*Three!*' I said.

'Egg-xactly! Cyril said. 'That's a good enough hat trick for me any day!'

Then he did his Cyril-dance again, with Miss Fellows, in case there was anyone who hadn't seen it. Mr Hope didn't Cyril-dance exactly, but he smiled and told all the little ones they should get our autographs, because Harpur and Cyril and I were ex-Red Row Stars, who were going to be famous.

Cyril was right. It wasn't the kind of hat trick I'd been hoping for, but it had got us into the Premier Division. I was in the team, not a Super-sub any more. I was scoring goals again and we were going to play in the Brontley League Premier Division and beat everybody out of sight and N. McCann was going to score millions and billions and trillions of Rocket Shot Wham-bam Super Goals, a whole Football Career Book full of them!

That would teach Miss Fellows a lesson!

relinq... post a... Reserve Team Manag...
United. David has given County sterling service over the...
player and later as a backroom boy. I am sure everyone at the Lane ...
him success in his new post.

ANOTHER SUCCESS

The 4–3 victory over Alyson Town in extra time which brought the Walsingham Floodlit Cup back to the Lane for the first time should not be allowed to overshadow the achievement of our Colts Squad under Manager Tommy Cowans. Our youngsters competed in the Western Area Qualifying Competition, finishing second, thereby earning a place in the Brontley League Premier Division for next season.

The issue remained in doubt until the last match, a creditable draw at the Lane with close rivals Queenstown. Two goals from promising striker Bernard 'Napper' McCann and one from defensive stalwart Cyril Small were enough to see us through, by virtue of our superior goal difference, as the league table below shows:

BRONTLEY LEAGUE

WESTERN AREA QUALIFYING COMPETITION FINAL TABLE

after Fifth Series Results

League Table	P	W	D	L	F	A	Pts	GD
Olympic YC	5	4	1	0	16	8	13	+8
Warne Colts	5	1	3	1	14	11	6	+3
Queenstown	5	1	3	1	9	8	6	+1
Hume	5	1	3	1	8	9	6	–1
Swanley	5	1	2	2	8	10	5	–2
Wolverton	5	0	2	3	6	15	2	–9

WARNE COUNTY COLTS APPEARANCES AND GOAL-SCORERS

Bantam 2, Scott 3, Brocken 5, Small 4(1), Fish 4+1s, Robinson 3+1s, Purdy 4, Brown 4, Jezz 5(4), Matthews 4+1s (1), Mole 4+1s, Singh 5 (3), McCann 2+2s (3), McCall 2 (1), Alexiou 3+2s, Smart 1. Opponents: OG I

Manager Tommy Cowans and his able back-up, 'Jumbo' Hope, are to be congratulated as much as the boys.

STOP PRESS! Colts' Goalie Tony Bantam has been selected to play for the Brontley League Representative side in the Cement Corporation Cup against Middleway and District. Despite his tender years Tony has already made his debut for the Reserves in a friendly, and he is obviously a 'Warney' to watch! ... Representative side was sel... from the pick of all twenty-four ... as taking ... ley League Qualifying C... the